WE DON'T HEAR CRICKETS ANYMORE

Kel Byron

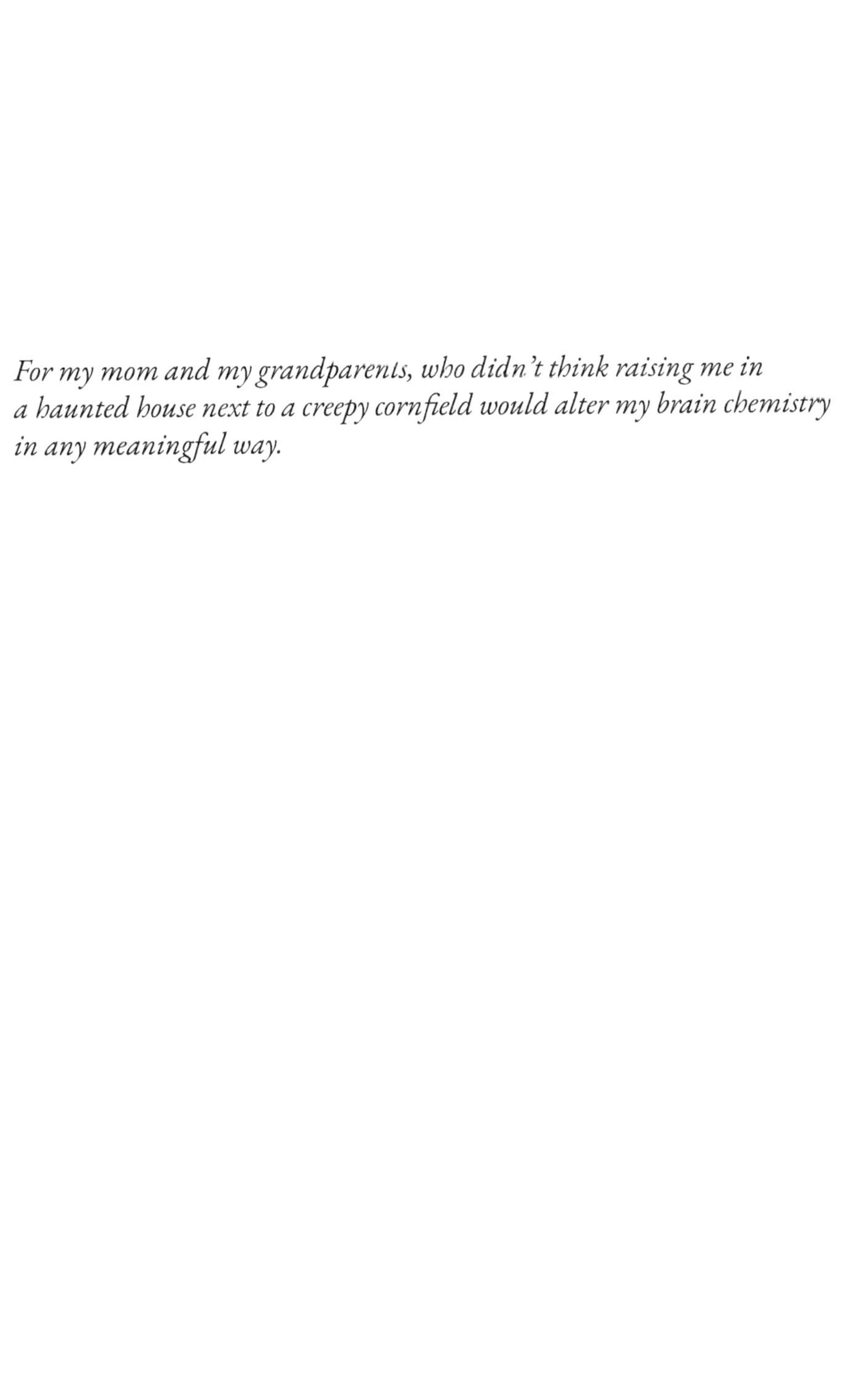

*For my mom and my grandparents, who didn't think raising me in
a haunted house next to a creepy cornfield would alter my brain chemistry
in any meaningful way.*

Table of Contents

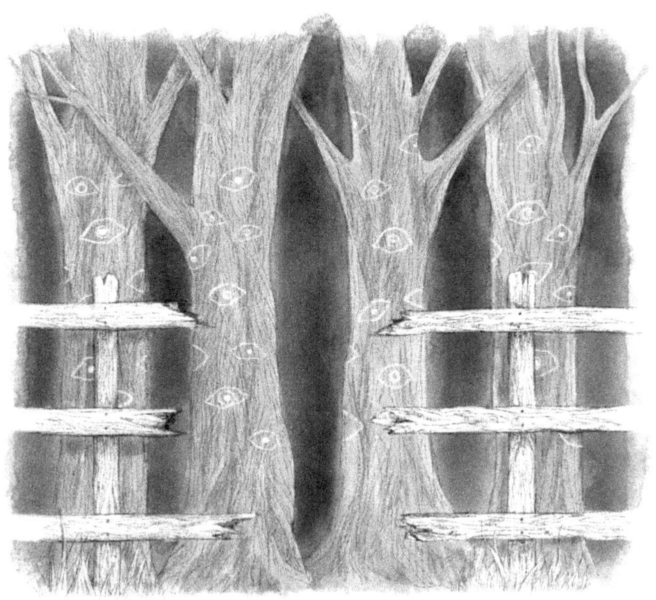

Trail Camera

Spencer's hunting blind, which he had built himself from the ground up, didn't get much use anymore. Two rounds of chemo and early-onset arthritis in both knees meant fewer long walks out to the woods, and less early mornings spent crouched in a pile of dead leaves and snow.

"Gone soft," as his friends said. They did it to tease him, knowing he didn't like the attention or the get-well cards and the little bell they rang on the last day of treatment. Instead of congratulating him on surviving cancer, they dragged his ass to the only bar in town, then asked when he was getting his hunting rifle out again. *"Not for a while"*, he told them. Nowadays, he watches the wildlife from a distance, creating faux intimacy with bird feeders by the windows and a trail camera hidden in a tree next to his hunting spot. *"Like an old woman,"* he joked.

The camera was the highlight of his days, even if he wouldn't admit it. He could pretend, if only for a short while, that he was tucked away in the bushes or mingling with the wildlife, unseen and inoffensive. Welcomed. It made him feel like a scientist. The images and videos showed rare, treasured sights: a great horned owl in flight, a mother doe with her fawn, a black bear discovering the bait Spencer had left behind. With no humans crouching in the hunting blind, nature had claimed the structure as part of its kingdom. More than once, Spencer had considered sharing some of his photos with magazines and newspapers, but it felt better to keep them to himself.

And with beauty came brutality. He'd catch an unfortunate mouse being carried off to a predator's nest, or a coyote feasting on a freshly-caught rabbit. Such was nature, such was the law of the land. But the pool of blood found on the floor of his hunting blind was new.

He saw it in person before he saw it on the camera footage. The walk out to the trail cam was a long journey for his sore legs, but he made it every few days so he could switch the SD card and put some bait out for the animals. Flies were circling. It smelled awful, like rotten fruit and a mouthful of pennies.

Spencer covered his nose with the collar of his coat. "What the hell?" he murmured to himself, groaning as he took a few uneasy steps up the ladder. His knees didn't like it, but he had to see for himself. The door was marked with scratches from thin claws, too small to be a fully-grown bear but too large to be a coyote. Drag marks the color of dried blood painted the floor, the walls, and the rungs of the ladder.

Whatever this animal was, it had left behind some bones, some fur, and the legs of a deer that didn't have enough meat to sate its hunger. It was just decayed enough to stain the floor of the blind, a fetid, syrupy liquid seeping through the cracks and into the soil where mushrooms were already abundant. Slow, like an IV drip.

It was three feet off the ground. The door had been locked, he was sure of it. What kind of bear would bother to use a ladder?

A layer of mist was sitting just above the grass when Spencer came trudging out of the woods, using a sturdy tree branch as a walking stick. He was winded, as he usually was. He heard the creak of his loose gate being rattled by a slow wind, but he didn't know when he'd get around to fixing the hinges. It was a little louder than usual — more pathetic, more desperate for attention. Maybe some animal had messed with it. Maybe one of his shithead neighbors from down the dirt road had backed their truck into it by accident. They wouldn't tell him if they did.

The family farmhouse, which had belonged to Spencer's older brother before he decided to take some automotive job in Milwaukee, still looked like it had in the mid-70s. A thin wood paneling, the color of wet cardboard, covered most of the walls. The living room floor, which extended into the dining room, was a navy blue with so many speckles that the stains blended seamlessly into the pattern. He kept old lamps, magazines, newspapers, mismatched dishes, and a lace tablecloth that had turned yellow from cigarette smoke. Even his computer, which sat on a hardwood desk heavy enough to leave permanent indents in the carpet, was an antique from the days when visiting the internet was a physical spot in the home.

On that fuzzy, faded screen, Spencer saw what happened in his hunting blind.

Midnight, four days earlier: something was moving around in the long grass, lurking close to the ground. He couldn't tell what it was, but it was long and crawling on its belly. The joints of its limbs would occasionally peek over the brush, thin and emaciated, but the animal seemed intent on staying as low as possible. Spencer saw two eyes alight in the camera's night vision.

One o'clock: birds scattered. In the middle distance, a deer was running frantically, tripping over its own legs. The animal that had been crawling around in the grass had moved off-screen, but its shape reappeared in the background every few moments as a tangle of limbs weaving between thick foliage.

One-ten: the trees shook. Spencer could almost catch the shadow of something large dropping from the tree and into the darkness, but it was too blurry to tell. The forest was too dense.

One-thirty: something finally moved near the hunting blind. A hunched creature, pale but mostly hidden behind the undergrowth, dragged a fresh kill toward the small shelter and began to climb with thin, long limbs. It pulled its meal behind it and lifted it without any physical stress. Through the windows of the blind, Spencer could see the creature's bony back as it feasted, the pale color of its flesh giving off a ghostly glow in the camera's light.

One-fifty: the beast left in a hurry. It didn't take anything when it went. It had finished its meal, bones and all.

It was probably some kind of sick, emaciated wolf or cougar,

Spencer thought. Maybe it had mange, maybe it was rabid. It was the only thing that made sense in his mind. He found himself trying to get away from that footage, not wanting to see it a second time, but he couldn't stop thinking about how he had only just been there less than an hour ago.

That chilling thought was interrupted by a sharp knock on his front door. He closed out of the video player and pulled himself away from the computer, pushing in his chair before slowly marching to his porch on sore, stiff legs. Through the window, he saw a familiar head of wispy gray hair hidden beneath a Detroit Lions cap.

"Hey," he greeted as the door swung open, offering his good friend Harry a tight handshake. "Been a while, huh?"

"Been too long." Harry gave Spencer a hard clap on the shoulder. Harry was about a head taller than Spencer and twice as broad, but he had been lucky with his health. Even at sixty, the man never stopped. He was dressed in work overalls and had a couple of big cardboard boxes sitting on the steps next to him. "You got a minute or two?"

Spencer backed up to let him inside the house. "Yeah, yeah, sure I do," he agreed. "How've you been? How's Charlotte?"

"She's doin' just fine," Harry said with a low chuckle. He grabbed the first cardboard box and carried it inside, all while pushing the second one into the house with his foot. "She's, uh ... spendin' some time at her sister's house downstate right now."

Spencer nodded, his eyes traveling from Harry's tired face down to the boxes he had brought, mentally trying to put the pieces together. He winced a little. "You ain't separating, are you?" he asked, trying to be careful with his words. "Is that...?"

Harry quickly shook his head. "No! No, no, not at all," he said. He spoke fast, banishing the thought. "We're fine. We're doing great. This is, um..." he took a long pause, digging around in the breast pocket of his shirt for a box of Marlboro's. "We're moving out of the area, actually. I've been cleaning up, trying to get rid of some shit we don't need anymore. I thought you could use some of this – gardening supplies, some spare tools, the works. I know you've been workin' hard on that sweet potato patch you've got."

Spencer blinked, taken aback by the news. Harry wouldn't just move and leave the family property behind. He built that pole barn himself, his parents were buried there, this old dirt road had been his whole life. He and his wife raised three boys in that house.

"Moving?" he asked, offering Harry a lighter when he noticed him searching for one. "Why the hell are you two moving? I thought you just finished fixin' up that new addition at the back of the house. Beautiful work, by the way."

Harry didn't respond immediately. He sat down at the dining room table, lighting up a cigarette. His hands shook. "Yeah, well, something came up. It was a tough decision, I promise."

"No kidding," Spencer sounded disappointed. His circle of friends was getting a lot smaller these days. Some had died, some moved away to live with their kids, some had retired and found new homes in warmer states. "Charlotte get transferred to another school district?"

Harry shook his head. "Nah, nothing like that," he said. "We just, uh, need a change of scenery, I think. Living out by these old woods isn't doin' it for us anymore. We're gonna head to the suburbs close to where Ricky and his wife are living now. You know, spend more time with the grandkids. Retire quietly when the time is right."

Spencer noticed the way Harry's fingers twitched, the way he breathed in the cigarette smoke a little too quickly. Even his words, chosen so delicately, were drenched in lies and half-truths. There was something frantic and uncomfortable about his posture, his hunched back, his alert eyes, and the way he chose to sit with his back to the window. He didn't usually sit in that spot.

"Harry," Spencer said in a slow, calm voice. "Did something happen?"

The air in the dining room felt heavier then. The scent of cigarette smoke lingered and mixed with something dusty, oppressive, and stale. The clock on the wall had never been quite as loud as it was in those ten seconds of silence. And when it struck on the hour, it made the sound of a robin's call. It had never made Harry jump before now.

"Yeah," he finally said, eyes wandering around the room in thought. He tapped his cigarette against an amber glass ashtray. Spencer didn't smoke anymore, but he kept it around for visitors. "Yeah, something happened. There's ... somebody stalking the house, I think."

"Shit," Spencer breathed. "You called the police?"

"Charlotte did a few times, yeah," Harry continued. He let out a slow, frustrated sigh. "They didn't find anything. Some broken twigs, a busted spot in the fence, but nothing an animal couldn't be responsible for. Still, I know what I saw. Dogs have been goin' wild in the middle of the night, wakin' Charlie up. I ignored it the first few times, but after a week, I couldn't stand it anymore. Stood there on the porch with a flashlight, and there he was. Tall, dirty, naked as the day he was born." He tapped the ashtray, his fingers clumsy. "There's a man in the woods."

The hair on the back of Spencer's neck was standing on end, tickling him under the collar of his shirt. He didn't want to believe that a man could be that frightening, to chase a family away from their home when Harry was more than capable of protecting it. But the look in his friend's eyes, the way his breath was shallow, the way his fingers tapped on the table with heightened anxiety ... he had his reasons for running.

"Are you shitting me?" Spencer asked, but the chuckle in his throat was weak and trembling. "You're joking, aren't you?"

"Not one bit," Harry said. And when he looked up at Spencer and met his eyes, he had never been more serious in his life.

After a long pause, filled with uneven breaths and the sounds of an old house settling, Harry turned his head to watch a bird peck at the feeder near the dining room window. "You ever see anything weird out there, when you're ... bird-watchin', or whatever it is you do?"

Spencer's head was immediately filled with images of his hunting blind and the mess he had found it in that morning. He didn't want to exaggerate, but he didn't want to lie to Harry either. "Sometimes," he said, trying to sound as casual as possible. "I've got a wolf or a black bear out there that learned how to use a ladder. Heh, imagine that. Critters out there are getting smarter all the time."

"They sure are," Harry responded in a low, uncharacteristlcally soft voice. He left it at that.

And for the next few minutes, neither of them knew what to say. Spencer watched the movement of Harry's eyes, examining his shaking fingers and the dark circles under his eyes that hadn't been there before. Harry, on the other hand, looked far away. He was in his own world, perhaps trapped in the past while taking in every last detail of this house and its memories.

"I'll see you around from time to time, won't I?" Spencer asked once Harry's cigarette was burned down to the butt.

Harry didn't answer right away. When he finally nodded, it was slow and uncertain. "Sure you will," he said, but Spencer knew it was probably a lie.

When the boxes were unpacked and the two old friends had taken a little tour around the garden, Harry finally decided it was time to leave. And this time, he gave Spencer a longer, tighter handshake than usual.

That night, after Spencer picked at his microwave dinner and fell asleep watching TV, he couldn't stop thinking about what Harry had said. *There's a man in the woods.* Spencer didn't believe him, sure, but it didn't stop him from noticing that the squeak of bats and the flutter of nocturnal birds were absent that night.

When the sun rose, it was hidden behind an overcast sky and gray, dreary clouds. Spencer made a pot of coffee right after dawn – decaf, for his failing heart. He ignored the fruit sitting in a basket on his countertop, opting for a granola bar for breakfast instead. Easy. Simple. With his coffee in hand and slippers on his aching feet, Spencer stepped out onto the porch to get some fresh air, making the slow walk to the mail box.

Nothing yet. The mailman was showing up later and later all the time. Spencer was about to shuffle back to his house when his eyes caught the busted gate, being pushed by the wind with a creak that made his ears sting. He'd fix those hinges later, he told himself. But he was surprised by the number of flies buzzing around the fence.

In the afternoon, Spencer went out to the only diner in town and ate a sandwich by himself, his company taking the form of a half-dozen regulars who stopped to ask the same questions – *how are you holding up? Do any hunting lately? Boy, that thunderstorm last week was somethin' else.*

He paid attention to the conversations that buzzed around him. His hometown was getting smaller. People stopped showing up to these old haunts. Even the waitress, who had been working there for years and used to be a good friend of Spencer's ex-wife, shook her head in disappointment when he asked if business had been good.

"Usually, it's busier than hell this time of year," she said, scribbling something on a tiny notepad and shoving it in her apron. "We've had our famous pumpkin pie on display all week – you know how quickly that used to sell."

"Yeah, I remember," Spencer smiled.

"Now, we're lucky if we can get rid of 'em by the end of the day," the waitress continued with a discontented sigh. "Town's gettin' smaller every year, Spence. I think our generation was the last hoo-rah."

The last hoorah. With old friends moving away and businesses going under, these small farming and logging towns just weren't what they used to be.

"Couple'a old friends of mine are leaving soon," Spencer said, fishing for a few extra dollars from his breast pocket for a tip. "I'm sure they aren't the only ones. It's real quiet in town, ain't it?"

"Quieter than ever," the waitress said. She looked out the

window, wistful and depressed, as her dark blue eyes wandered over the decals they had put up to get in the Thanksgiving spirit. Those stupid cartoon turkeys and pumpkins looked pathetically cheery. "The Schroeders are leaving too."

"Ben and Molly?" Spencer asked from behind his coffee cup. Decaf.

"That's right," the woman continued while wiping her hands on a well-worn cloth. "Moving a couple towns over to a smaller place, I guess. They said the house was just too big now that their boy is off to college. But–" she paused, scratching the back of her neck beneath a puffy blonde nest, stiff with hairspray. "Molly was real jittery about it when she showed up to book club. Panicky, I mean. I dunno, maybe that old house was haunted."

She laughed at that, the idea ridiculous to both her and Spencer. But Spencer still couldn't help the way his eyes darted down the bar, hoping no one saw the brief hint of worry that passed over his finely-crafted mask.

After Spencer paid for his meal and promised the staff he'd be back in a couple of days, he decided to take the long way home and look at sights he hadn't seen in a while. It was that time of year when they were cutting the corn, leaving the fields dry and shockingly bare after the tall, yellow stalks had been blocking the view for so long. Most of the main road was the same as it had always been, interrupted only by the rare empty building or store closed early for the day. But once Spencer reached the edge of town where the village blocks turned to fields and trees, it all felt so empty. So cold.

The little yellow house had a 'for sale' sign out front. The old widow who lived there used to have a beautiful garden with archways and rose bushes, but it was neglected now. The family two doors down had already left, and the swingset where their twins used to play was removed. It left a patch of dirt behind where their shoes had dragged over yellow grass. A barn had been demolished. Sidewalks were overgrown. Spencer drove further out into the country, passing by the cemetery where his own parents were buried, noticing that the branches hadn't been cleaned up after the last big thunderstorm.

He thought about his weak knees, his aching legs, his thinning hair. He thought about how often Harry coughed these days, and about the waitress at the diner and how wrinkled her hands were despite the bright pink nailpolish that kept her feeling young. Maybe this was the last hoorah after all. And when these families were gone and those houses were empty, the moss and wildlife would reclaim all of this.

His old Chevy got him home, but not without the engine light blinking the whole way. Spencer told himself he'd deal with it later – the same excuse he used for everything. His annoyance only reached new levels when he pulled up to his gate and saw that the hinges weren't just loose anymore. The whole damn thing had been torn off and was lying on the ground now, splintered bits of wood surrounding it. "Son of a bitch," he said hoarsely under his breath. That repair would have to happen sooner rather than later.

That trip from the car to the shed to the gate was like running five miles, and by the time he plopped down on a stump to catch his breath, his legs were already shaking. He thought about the demolished barn again while looking at his own thin, frail limbs. He thought about the overgrown garden while considering whether or not he'd try to clean his messy house tonight. His hometown had cancer, too.

The flies were still abundant. He swatted them away, sputtering when one flew too close to his lips. The cold air made his nose stuffy, but he could still pick up the faint scent of something rancid and sour. Metallic. He followed the thickest cloud of insects with his eyes, following the length of the fence until he spotted a stain on the wood. The fence was scuffed, either by claws or antlers, and Spencer could imagine a buck trying to scratch an itch. But the bits of fur scattered in the dirt told a different story.

Something had died over there, he could tell. There were coyotes out at night. Foxes. Hell, maybe even a bobcat could be out there. He crinkled his nose in disgust at the smell, but decided to leave the scattered bits of fur and bone. There was no telling what kinds of germs were all over that thing.

When Spencer opened up his toolbox and began the slow process of putting the gate back where it belonged, he couldn't keep his eyes off the woods. The trees were shivering in the autumn breeze, fragile and thin. The way they groaned every time the wind passed through was haunting. Nature's windchimes. And still, his mind was stuck on what Harry had said to him.

There was a man in the woods.

He chided himself for falling victim to what he was sure was baseless paranoia, but the goosebumps on his skin and the way his eyes darted at every shadow didn't agree. He thought about the blood on the floor of his hunting blind and the animal bones and fur left scattered in the soil. It would take more than a rabid animal to chase him away from his property. He wasn't jumpy like that.

It was just animals. It was just nature. There wasn't a man in the woods.

Trying to fix up the gate with an aching back and two bum knees didn't make for a quick or easy process. Spencer found himself wishing he had a helping hand. Maybe if he had stayed married and had kids like Harry, he'd have a bigger support system. He'd have someone to take care of him when he got old and feeble. That's what community was supposed to be, right? Friends, neighbors, a whole system of good, small-town folks willing to lend a hand. The uneasy reality was that Spencer was alone, and with his friends leaving the area and following new dreams in their retirement age, he would only get lonelier.

"Fuckin' thing…" he grumbled to himself as he fought with a stubborn, rusty screw. He sat up on his knees, brushing off his hands on the thighs of his jeans. Twigs snapped and leaves crinkled, a pile of autumn debris getting strewn about near the treeline. Spencer squint-ed to get a better view. Probably a squirrel or a muskrat. He got back to work, surprised that the sound of his drill didn't scare off whatever critter was burrowing in the fallen leaves.

He fixed everything up just after sunset, his eyes burning from squinting too much in the dark. He trudged back home, breathless and leaning on his cane.

That night, he locked his door the moment he got back inside *– for no reason, he told himself.* It was just good practice. He made a pot of spaghetti with too many noodles, the bottom of the dish burn-ing a little when he found himself staring out the window for too long. The trees were moving an awful lot, but the weathervane on top of his shed hardly budged. The wind chimes on the porch voiced the softest, faintest jingle. It was a nostalgic and mournful sound.

And while washing the dishes, Spencer looked out the kitchen window to watch the long grass sway in the wind. All the stars were out. It was a half-moon. And at the edge of the woods where the field met the trees, Spencer saw a set of antlers. An old buck, its eyes shimmering under dim moonlight, stared at him from a distance as if it had been watching him the whole time.

He stared back, expecting the beast to break eye contact and start running back into the woods. It didn't. Spencer whispered something under his breath about *'strange animals lately'* and closed the curtains tightly. Something about those dark, shiny eyes made him feel uncomfortably exposed.

He had heard about diseases that spread among deer and other animals. Wasting diseases. Rabies. That night, he got a phone call from his sister up in Marquette. She had a daughter who worked with animals.

"Does Elise come across a lot of critters with rabies?" he asked.

His sister, Jacqueline, made a thoughtful noise before speaking. "Once in a while," she said. "Why? You didn't bring in another mangy stray cat, did you?"

Spencer chuckled, recalling fond memories of friendly barn cats and the litter of kittens he helped rehome a couple years ago. He wasn't the type of guy to have a pet in the house, but he couldn't deny that he enjoyed seeing those kittens tumble around on the porch.

"Not exactly," he answered. "Somethin' was in my hunting blind a few nights ago. Real scrawny, hairless thing – it left a big mess behind and I figured maybe some wasting disease was going 'round the wolf population out here."

Even though he couldn't see Jacqueline, Spencer could hear the shiver in her voice and imagined her making a face of disgust. "That's a bit spooky," she said. "I don't think rabies would make its hair fall out, though. But if you see any animals walking around in circles, drooling, getting real aggressive ... call up animal control and don't touch it, okay?"

Spencer chuckled at his sister's concern. "I ain't stupid enough to touch a wild animal," he said. "Although, I'd rather die of rabies than go through another round of chemo."

"Oh, don't say things like that," his sister chided. "You're lucky I'm not there in person or I'd slap those last three hair off your bald head." Judging by the smile in her voice, she could tell he was joking.

Most nights were the same for Spencer. He turned on the TV, watched some local news channel, sometimes flipping over to college football or baseball if the season permitted. It was brainless background noise to lull him into a sense of relaxation, less stimulating than a good book but better than silence. Before long, he'd fall asleep in his recliner, a warm quilt over his lap and the remote control in one hand. Tonight, nothing changed, except for the gentle tapping on Spencer's window that roused him from his sleep just an hour after midnight.

"Hm?" he sat up mid-snore, his mouth hanging open and his throat dry. He rubbed his forehead with a delirious mumble as he lowered the footrest on his chair. "What the hell?"

Spencer pushed himself up, legs still wobbly, and caught himself on the coffee table when he started to stumble. One foot was still half-asleep, and the pins and needles made him wince. In the moments that it took for him to grab his cane and head toward the kitchen, limping a little from the numbness, he heard it again: a gentle tapping at the window, three times in a row. The only other sound in the house was the slow tick of the bird clock on his wall – the same one that had startled the hell out of Harry the day before. It was muted and soft now, voicing the chirp of an oriole. One o'clock.

"Who's–?" Spencer began to say, before he noticed the shadow cast against the curtain. He could see the outline of it clear as day, illuminated by the porch light: a huge head, messy fur, and sharp, curled antlers with four points on either side. It didn't move. It didn't make a sound. But the buck remained, as still as stone, looming behind that curtain as if waiting for Spencer to let it in.

"Go on, shoo!" Spencer said, waving his cane in the air. The beast didn't move, it didn't twitch, and it didn't make a sound.

His blood ran cold at the mere concept of this thing knowing that he was inside. Did it hear him? Did it see him through a gap in the fabric? That feeling only became more chilling when the shadow finally began to move. It stepped, slowly and deliberately, until it disappeared from the kitchen window and moved left. Spencer could hear the path it took. The porch floorboards creaked with each step until that buck was at his front door instead, one of its cold black eyes visible through a gap in the lace curtain.

"Go!" Spencer tapped his cane against the wall, hoping the sudden tap would startle the beast. "Get outta here! Freaky thing..."

But the buck didn't leave. It stayed rooted to the spot, its eyes dark and cold as if no life existed behind them. Spencer could hear the low, rough grunt of its voice, breathing heavily just behind the glass.

The thing was panting, eager, and desperate. It wanted in.

And with one last grunt of frustration, the buck tilted its head against the little square window, its antlers hitting the glass with a loud, piercing scrape. Spencer jumped, a chill passing between his shoulders. The beast did it again, harder this time, making a low sound of exertion as it used its full weight to make the door tremble. This house was old. Those locks were original. Spencer could see the stress it caused against the latch.

In a rush, Spencer stepped back and stumbled over his own feet, making a dash to his bedroom. His cane was abandoned somewhere on the way, clattering to the worn wood floor. He threw open the closet doors and tossed aside a pile of clothes he hadn't worn in years, finding the edges of a long gun case covered in a thin layer of dust. He popped open the clasps, pulled a hunting rifle out with shaky hands, and loaded it while he limped back to the kitchen. His lungs were on fire when he got there and his head was pounding, but the deer was gone.

In those few moments, it had stalked away. Only the jingle of the wind chimes and the soft crinkle of tumbling leaves remained. Spencer could hear his own pulse in his ears, rhythmic and deep. It made him squeamish. And for the next hour, he sat in his recliner with his hunting rifle on his lap, keeping the lights off and the curtains open. The beast didn't come back.

When morning came, Spencer unlocked the door and stepped outside with heavy circles beneath his eyes and jaws that were sore from grinding his teeth all night. That first step into the cold autumn air made the hair on his arms prickle. He grimaced when he became aware of a rancid smell, noticing the dry, dead leaves rolling across the porch and over dark stains that weren't there the day before. The stink was carried on a cold breeze.

In the daylight, he felt alone there. Nothing was watching him from the treeline, no traffic passed by on that old dirt road, and the wind was still quiet. And yet, he shuddered with dread and frustration when he noticed what had become of his fence. This time around, the gate had been spared, but something had made its own door. The damage was rough and splintered. Judging by the way the debris had scattered, something had forced its way in from the other side.

Most animals could jump over, he thought. If they tried hard enough, they could even squeeze between the wooden planks. Whatever burst through the fence did so out of sheer rage and brute strength, leaving thick, stinking bloodstains in its wake. The blood was dark brown in color and mostly dried, but flies were still attracted to the flattened grass that made a path from the forest to Spencer's front door.

Spencer called up Harry first, but he didn't answer. Then he tried Animal Control after breakfast, sitting down at the kitchen table with his back to the window. "Think I got a rabid deer out here," he said after giving his address. "There's blood on my porch and it was circlin' around my house most of the night. That's usual for rabies, ain't it? Confusion, walking in circles? The damn thing busted down a section of my fence too."

He made the report, feeling a small bit of relief in knowing that someone would be out in a few hours to search the area. Spencer couldn't get his mind off of it. He didn't want to leave the house, he didn't want to go to town, even watching the birds didn't take his mind off of what he had seen. What he had felt. The birds and squirrels were less abundant that day.

He hadn't felt that kind of sickening dread since he found blood all over his hunting blind. It was that thought — that connection – that made him remember the trail camera still out there in the woods, probably ready for a change of batteries. Spencer's heart raced a little when he imagined having to go out there, but he was a realistic man. Maybe he caught the deer on camera. Maybe evidence would help. Maybe he'd shoot the damn thing himself and put this entire problem to rest.

Fear was what ran Harry and Charlotte out of their home. But for Spencer, what he wanted were results.

With his mind made up, he packed up his rifle case and put it on his back, grabbing a polished wooden walking stick for the trip. It was daylight. The sun was shining. For all he knew, that dying deer had probably already found a hole to crawl into, and he'd find its carcass covered in flies and maggots.

The walk out to the blind was long and damp, the ground still slightly muddy from the heavy rains they had been getting all week. Spencer felt claustrophobic. A strong scent of mildew and ozone was stuck in the air. Despite his discomfort and the insistent feeling of being watched, he rarely saw any signs of life in the woods that morning – a squirrel ran into its burrow far ahead on the path, a few birds scattered, and worms rose to the surface, but it wasn't long before Spencer didn't see anything at all.

But when he reached that rickety little hunting blind, the dread truly sank in. It smelled like a sun-bloated corpse. The woodland floor was flattened, bits of fur and bone scattered around, and the flies were gathering in droves. Spencer made a sound of disgust as he saw the maggots underneath his shoes, the wiggling mass attracted to the scent of death and the blood soaked into the soil. There was no body, no flesh. And yet, he felt as if he had stepped on hallowed ground.

This wasn't here before. This was fresh. He had a sinking suspicion that whatever had made its home in his hunting blind had brought back another meal.

Spencer was quick about grabbing the SD card from his camera and putting the fresh one in. His hands shook slightly, uncomfortable and cold, and he almost couldn't get away from the blind fast enough. This time, he didn't look inside – he didn't want to know what dripped from between the floorboards.

But as he began to walk away, one slow step at a time with his walking stick dug into the mud, he heard a low grunt and a soft shuffle. Something was still in there. The wooden boards creaked, whining against the weight of something just a little too big to fit. Spencer didn't look back, but he paused. He stood still.

Another grunt, a little louder this time. It was almost like a bark, coming from the throat of an animal he couldn't name. The way its voice projected, clear and chilling, made Spencer wonder if the animal was trying to get his attention. Trying to convince him to turn around and come back, as if meeting his eyes was an unspoken challenge.

He didn't. He couldn't will himself to turn. When he heard the crunch of twigs behind him, he began to walk again, his chest tight and his breath weak with every wheeze and cough. The smell was starting to make him dizzy. Something still followed him, keeping the same pace as if watching in patient curiosity, and it carried that horrible smell with it. Step after step, Spencer could only breathe in the suffocating scent of fresh rot.

He walked a little faster, his eyes focused on the light filtering between the trees, and ignored the constant shiver of cold air against the back of his neck like the last breath of a corpse.

The feeling persisted, even when he was back in the safety of his home. The smell of sour blood was stuck in his nose, the vision of that deer staring through a gap in the curtains... It convinced him to lock the doors and lower the blinds, feeling no comfort even in the daylight. Was that what he had become? Afraid of his own home, shut out from nature, avoiding the thing he once loved the most? The woods, the first day of hunting season, even his little sweet potato garden – it brought him joy in an otherwise lonely, dull life. Now, it felt like it belonged to something else.

He rolled the SD card over in his palm, gnarled fingers carefully pushing it into his computer tower. For a moment, he wasn't sure he wanted to know what was on it. He hesitated. But after a few minutes of sitting at his desk with his hands on his head and the clock ticking rhythmically to break the silence, he opened the files one at a time.

His fingers tapped against the desk. Hesitant. Nervous. And as the first video began to play, he stretched the window on his desktop to get a better look at the harsh, grainy image on the screen.

At nine o'clock, there was a rustling in the bushes and a possum waddled across the camera view, minding its own business.

Spencer found his heart lightening just a little at the way it burrowed in the leaves, probably coming back to its den after grabbing a snack from his garbage can. He didn't mind. He spotted a few birds heading back to their nests for the night, reminding him that some things were still normal out there.

At ten o'clock, everything was eerily still. The push and pull of the wind made the tree branches shiver, but his only visitors were a few flying insects that caught the camera's night vision lens, glowing white and green in the darkness. Up close, they looked like alien things, wings moving too fast to see with twisted little legs and antennae. Spencer's heart started to race. Something felt different now.

And at eleven o'clock, Spencer watched as an old deer walked slowly into view, four points on either side of its antlers. His pounding heart started to thump to the point of pain when he saw those shiny black eyes, familiar but different. Something was strange about them. The deer stopped to dig its face around in the leaves and grass, blinking every so often and swishing its tail. It was old and white around the muzzle, but its eyes were bright and alert. Healthy.

It padded at the ground a little, shaking its antlers to knock the bugs away. Five minutes later, the buck turned its head, on edge and ready to run. He could practically sense the way its fur stood on end, watching a shiver pass through its body even on a grainy screen. Spencer observed with bated breath, inching closer to the monitor. The buck's ears twitched. It stood frozen in place. And then, both the animal and Spencer jumped at the same time as something rushed through the trees so quickly that it only appeared as a blurry flash of white flesh. It leapt into the air and landed on the deer's back, its weight toppling the beast over to pin it to the ground. The buck flailed and fought, collapsed to the forest floor in a tangle of limbs.

The creature was a man – a man with long, wiry limbs and pale skin, suctioned close to his bones and stretched over a long and gaunt body. His eyes were wide and dark, reflecting the light of the camera as he overpowered the deer with ease. Spencer put a hand over his mouth, pushing his chair away from his desk as he watched the man grab hold of the buck's antlers and twist its head enough to break its neck in one powerful motion. The deer seized and twitched, limbs shaking like a spider in water, before going limp.

Spencer was trembling and a cold sweat broke out on his forehead as he watched the man crawl over the deer's body. His spindly limbs barely looked human, thin and powerful at the same time. His arms were too long. His joints and his flexibility didn't make sense. The man crouched over the deer's torso and took a powerful hold on its antlers, saliva dripping from his mouth with impatient hunger. He pulled once, twice, and then a third time, until he tore its head straight from its shoulders with a spray of blood and steam. Spencer felt his stomach twist with nausea, thankful that he couldn't hear the sound it must have made.

When the man tossed the deer's head to the side, he crouched down by the gaping, torn stump of its neck and began to taste the fresh blood. His tongue was impossibly long. It slid out from between blunt, crooked teeth and twisted itself around the deer's exposed spine, savoring the heat of his kill. It wasn't enough to just bite and tear at the flesh. He broke off a limb and his jaw unhinged to swallow it whole, his throat stretching like a snake. Spencer couldn't move. He couldn't look away. He watched, horrified and disgusted, as the man devoured his prey one piece at a time, leaving only–

The head.

Midnight. The man finished his meal, now covered in blood and shaking with satisfaction. His huge, thin hands reached for the deer's head. Its eyes were wide and glassy, empty of all feeling, and its swollen tongue lolled out of its mouth. Heavy. Wet. Spencer recognized that lifeless stare and the dampness of its fur, sticking out in all directions as it began to grow cold.

And then, the man dug – he dug around inside of its flesh and bone, pulling out bits of its spine and muscle, shoveling some of its tissue into his gaping mouth while letting the rest fall into messy piles on the ground. Spencer had to hold back his nausea while watching the man's twisted art project come to life. When the man was satisfied with what he had done, the hollowed-out carcass was slowly pulled over his head, dripping and twitching. He positioned it snugly on his shoulders until it formed a gruesome, terrible mask.

He stood there for a while, breathing heavily. Spencer watched his chest move as adrenaline coursed through his monstrous body, standing even taller now than before. And for the longest time, he stared at the screen while the dead, black eyes of the buck caught the trail camera's light. In that moment, Spencer knew that the man was aware of him: his blind, his camera, his home. His posture felt like a challenge. A threat.

When he slowly began to walk away, dripping blood and twitching like a rabid beast fighting for control of its own limbs, Spencer had never felt so scared or empty in his life.

He sat in his office chair for close to an hour, fingers clutching the edge of the desk tightly. That face was still trapped in his memory: empty, bloody, limp. His phone began to ring as someone from

Animal Control called him back, but he didn't answer. He let it go to voicemail, his eyes starting to gloss over in shock.

He'd call Harry later and tell him he was right. Maybe he'd head to the diner to see if anyone was interested in buying some of the gardening supplies he didn't need anymore, so long as he got home before nightfall. He'd lock the place up tight for a night or two. That heavy dining room table would lean up nicely against the door, he thought. He had a hammer and nails in the basement.

His phone began to ring again, the sound blending with the tinkle of windchimes from the other side of his window. Spencer's eyes were too focused on the distant treeline to notice.

That broken fence still needed fixing, he realized. But that was a job for the next person.

Before the Last Stop

I missed my grandfather. He was still with us, but I missed the person he used to be: funny, talkative, sharp, and full of joy. Alzheimer's had locked his personality behind brief sparks of activity, surrounded by days of quiet, agitated boredom. Some days, he still remembered stories from before I was born, or regaled me with tales of how he met my grandmother. Most days, though, he was just angry.

He was having one of his good days, and I just so happened to be having a terrible one. I came to visit him after my morning classes were done, my leather messenger bag still on my shoulder, tilting my weight to one side. My eyes were red and puffy from a sleepless night. For now, my phone was on silent; every time I heard that little *ding*, I found myself hoping and praying that it was her. Megan. I wasn't handling the transition from 'girlfriend' to 'stranger' very well, and a night of arguing and begging for answers didn't make it any better.

I looked at the last messages I sent to her, feeling humiliated by my own late-night desperation.

I'm sorry I yelled at you. Please don't give up on me yet. I want us to work out. I'm trying so hard.

The distraction of constantly checking my phone forced me to tuck it away altogether, hoping that putting her out of sight would truly make her disappear. It didn't work.

My grandfather, as delirious as he was in his home hospice bed, noticed something was wrong when an hour passed and I said nothing. One of his weak, wrinkled hands waved toward me as if trying to pat my shoulder, but missing by a mile. I put my hand over his on the bed, being careful of his paper-thin skin.

"Yer outta sorts today, Jeannie," he croaked while signaling for me to hand him a styrofoam cup full of room-temperature tap water. My name wasn't Jeannie, but I wasn't going to correct him. Jeannie was what he called my mom. I'd let him believe I was her for a day if it meant sparing him the misery of knowing she had died the year before.

"I'm alright," I assured him. "Just didn't sleep too well, is all. How are you feeling today?"

My grandfather groaned as he stretched out his legs beneath the blankets. His skin was dry and flaky. He needed lotion and some toenail clippers, but I reminded myself to take care of that later.

"Sore as hell," he finally answered, shifting his feet with a wince. "Muscles hurt from workin' a 14-hour shift yesterday. Only took one break for my lunch, can you believe that?"

"14 whole hours, huh?" I asked, voicing a soft, awkward chuckle. Grandpa went back to his masonry days often, talking about houses he helped build and important pieces of local history. His favorite job, and the one he remembered the most vividly, was the reconstruction of our hometown's train station. It was a beautiful building made of red brick and rounded archways, but it had since been turned into office rentals after the grain elevator stopped running.

No one rented them anymore. The town was just too small and businesses were moving out. In his mind, however, that train station was still in its glory days.

"How much longer until it's done?" I asked him. Anything to keep him in a place where he felt peace.

He responded with a dreamy, toothless smile. "Oh, we're almost there," he said. "Then we're puttin' new doors on, stained glass windows... It's gonna be a beauty, that's for sure."

He was right. It was a beauty. That was one of the few blessings about my grandfather's condition. He lived in a world where his modern marvel was never finished, where his pride lived on, and those stories never got old or stale. It was an illusion I never wanted to break, gladly resigned to letting him hold that little piece of heaven tight to his chest.

"You're gonna have to give me a tour when it's finished up," I said, and he smiled wider at that. "Show me all the little secrets and your favorite parts."

"I'm gonna do just that, Jeannie," he said as he patted my hand. "I'm gonna do just that. And when the station's built, we're gonna sit out there in the evening and watch the trains go by. You, me, and your mama. They got one comin' from outta Cleveland that moves faster than hell, you know that? The one that only travels at night."

I raised my brows and shook my head with interest. He had told me about this train before – *the Black Bullet*, he called it – but he hadn't mentioned it in months. Those stories were a relic of the time before he started to lose himself.

"I didn't know that," I told him. "It's real fast, huh?"

"So fast the devil can't catch it," he chuckled, and I saw that twinkle in his eyes again. In that moment, reminiscing about a ghost story he used to tell when I was a toddler on his knee, it was like having him back. "We're gonna sit out there right after sunset, make some lemonade, and we're gonna listen for the whistle, Billie-girl. You always loved hearin' the whistle coming."

It was a shock to hear my real name come from his mouth after so long. Growing up, he never called me Bianca or Bee. It was always Billie. *His* Billie-girl. And now, as he said that name and looked me in the eyes with an expression of pride and satisfaction, I knew that years of our lives came rushing back to him all at once, if only for a moment or two. He called me Billie and he really, truly, completely meant it.

"I'm gonna hold you to that," I told him with another squeeze of his delicate, cold finger bones. It was hard not to wear my sorrow on my face.

He just nodded with a sense of certainty, squeezing my hand back with half the strength. Moments later, when he started to drift off to sleep, I could only hope he was dreaming about his best days by those train tracks.

When I checked my phone, I was disappointed to see messages from everyone except her. This was the most crowded form of loneliness, being greeted by a barrage of attention but caring about none of it. The girl who sat next to me in ART 214 wanted to know if I was going to a Halloween party that weekend. Aunt Loretta was asking if I had any old photos of my mom to use for a scrapbook. All I cared about was Megan's name in my contacts and the messages left abandoned hours ago.

Deep down, I knew she wouldn't respond. I knew my plea fell on deaf ears: to try again, to be more attentive, to move around my schedule just for her.

She was moving to the West Coast and transferring to a different university. She said it would be a dream to take me with her, to have our own little apartment full of house plants and cramped, cozy spaces. While she went to school to be a vet, I'd be doing hair or selling my art at coffee shops. I would do it in a heartbeat if I could. That's what I told her. But when she asked who would take care of my grandfather, my lack of an answer gave her everything she needed to know. She couldn't wait for me forever.

The hours ticked by as I did my homework in the corner of the room, my grandfather's weak, dry snore accompanying the art history paper I was trying to write. It all felt worthless, really. I wouldn't pass. I had already dropped two classes to make time for this, all because the majority of my family refused to get involved. Now and again, they called to ask if he was still alive. But they didn't want to see Grandpa like this, overshadowing their memory of him when his mind was quick and his body was healthy.

I was twenty-two, watching opportunities fly away from me while I stood tethered to the ground, trying desperately to spread my wings without success. Why was it okay for me to stay trapped here, but not them? Why did I have to pay the price?

My grandfather would never know how many hours I spent in this spot. He'd never know how often I imagined giving up and being born again. I'd have a new name, a new brain, a new family, parents who were still alive, and hope for a future that was endless. I didn't like this life because it didn't feel like mine. Maybe the next one would stick. Maybe the next one would feel right.

But before I went anywhere, I had a photography project I wanted to finish. It was one of the few things I still believed in – one of the few things I had confidence in anymore. That day, while talking to my grandfather, I got a jolt of inspiration that would set me on the right track. I knew what I needed to do. It meant the world to see the way his eyes lit up as he described that train, bathed in black paint and moving so fast against the horizon that it was just a blur. *So fast the devil can't catch it.* Even if the old train station was closed down and the tracks were barely used anymore, I could do something with that idea as a final parting gift. To him. To me. To my hometown.

"I'm going out for a while," I said to him, but he didn't respond. He was still asleep. "Leona's gonna come sit with you until dinner, then I'll be back. When she gets here, you tell her that story you told me, alright?"

He let out a rattling snore, shallow and slow. His breaths were getting further apart, but I wasn't sure if it was the weakness of his lungs or how deeply he slept.

When my Aunt Leona and Uncle Cal showed up, they bitched and moaned about how bad the timing was, as I knew they would. It was that gentle, friendly kind of guilt tripping. *We really don't mind helping, but you know how busy things are.* I walked out the moment they started yapping about the charity barbecue they were missing down in the church parking lot. The drama of it all.

But despite my annoyance, the air was fresh and crisp. The sky was overcast and the leaves were just starting to fall from the trees. It was a perfect day, a soft breeze passing through dying yellow grass and cornfields that were almost ready to harvest. I took a few photos on my way there: deer in the distance, a barn falling to pieces with a hint of sunlight peeking through the clouds. I hated that the nostalgic beauty of this place wasn't enough to keep me there, to make me fall in love with my hometown the way I was when I was small. That's how I knew this feeling was real. Even when I tried to capture all the beauty around me, it wasn't good enough.

Little town that it was, my journey to the train tracks didn't go unseen. Chase, a kid I went to grade school with who never really flew the coop, pulled his busted red truck off to the side of the road when he saw me out there with my camera and tripod. I watched him toss his hat into the driver's seat, squinting into the wind. A part of me wanted to ignore him, tell him I was too busy to talk. But before I had that chance—

"Bee! Hey!" Chase called out, giving a sharp wave over the top of his head that looked more like a salute. "Hey, you're back in town. Thought you were off to college."

"I was," I said, giving him an awkward nod with a curled top lip. I softened my expression the moment I noticed his eyebrows shoot up in misunderstanding. "I mean, I still am. Just stopping by to see family."

It was a half-truth, and it was all I was willing to give him. I stopped by every day to *"see family"*, sometimes spending the night dozing off in the armchair near my grandfather's bed when he was afraid to wake up alone. For the life of me, I couldn't figure out why I was ashamed to tell Chase about all that. Maybe I just didn't want the questions or the sympathy. I got enough of that already.

I sat down on the creaking remains of an old wooden bench, leaving enough room so that Chase could sit next to me. We always got along decently in school, despite having nothing in common. We were both different, you see. In a graduating class of fewer than sixty kids, his autism diagnosis and my status as the only black girl in our grade meant we often inhabited the same corner table at lunch, somewhere between the anime kids and the one quiet goth girl who liked to draw.

But Chase was good. He was sweet, albeit relentlessly extroverted.

"You still working at the meat market?" I asked, flipping through some of the photographs I had already taken. None of them captured what I really wanted.

"Nah," Chase said. One of his legs was bouncing. "I'm at the hardware store now."

"Moving up in the world," I teased, but felt like an ass immediately after the words left my lips. "Sorry, that sounded sarcastic."

"No, no, you're good," Chase waved away the thought with a scrawny hand, knuckles slightly stained from grease. "I like it. I get to talk to folks about tools and fixin' cars all day. Sometimes I even make a few sales for spare parts. It's nice."

It sounded nice. The way the bounce in his leg transformed

from a nervous fidget to a jitter of gleeful excitement told me every-thing I needed to know about why he stayed. He was content here. When no one else would carve out a place for him to belong, he built it by himself. And despite the minimum wage job and the duct tape on his truck, I could tell that he was proud. Happy, even.

We sat side-by-side in silence for a good, long while, listening to the whistle of wind and the way it made the branches and corn stalks shiver with a dry sound. Somewhere around the block, a neigh-bor's dog was barking at a group of kids on bikes. Chase was still bouncing his leg, faster now. Less rhythmic and more anxious.

"I was at your mom's funeral," he said to break the silence. "Last July. The service was really nice."

"We don't have to talk about it," I explained.

Chase shrugged, letting out a shaky breath. "I know I didn't say anything to you then, but it just seemed like I should--"

"It's okay," I said. And while my expression was stiff, my tone of voice was as gentle as I could make it. "Really, it's ... it's fine. I know."

He dropped the subject with a deflated sigh, the tension washing out of his bony shoulders beneath a stained gray t-shirt. My mom's death was big news when it happened: her tiny sedan versus a semi truck. They had to replace the stop sign that got twisted from the impact, and that vibrant, brand new red was a constant reminder of the accidental landmark she had left behind. The grass never grew the same in that spot.

As a little kid, I cried at the thought of my mom dying one day. I thought it would be quiet and slow, paired with the beep of life support and the warmth of a wrinkled old hand. Death would arrive for her gently, and she would die smiling, with her parents waiting for her on the other side. Instead, she was buried in pieces. Tiny, mangled, broken pieces. It was a mercy that her father would never know.

I missed her with something that was more than grief. I know they say that grief is "love persevering", but I didn't feel like I carried her love with me anymore. It was something else: a horror concocted of anger, emptiness, and jealousy. Losing her felt like watching the last lifeboat float away, miles from the nearest shore. It was a betrayal without hope of repair, without forgiveness. Utter abandonment.

"I guess a few people from our graduating class are coming back for a bonfire party next weekend," Chase said while scratching the back of his neck. "I mean, if you wanna come by, I'm sure it'll be a good time. I'd like to see you there."

There was something desperate in his tone that told me this wasn't really about a bonfire. It was a quiet, delicate plea to stay when I think he could tell all I wanted was to disappear forever.

"I'll be out of town," I said. No explanation, no details.

Chase just nodded. "Yeah, okay, that's ... that's fine," he said. It wasn't fine. But when he cleared his throat and clapped his hands against his knees, I knew he wasn't going to fight about it. "Listen, I gotta go help my dad at the car wash, but if you're around tomorrow, maybe we can get lunch or something? If you're not – you know – out of town."

My chest felt tight. My lungs felt smaller, as if something in the air had shriveled them up inside of me mid-breath. "Yeah," I told him with a hesitant, fake smile. "Yeah, if I'm not out of town."

I watched him walk away, looking back only once to give me a slow, tentative wave and an awkward smile. In a very real way, it felt like saying goodbye to my childhood. He would carry on, planting his roots in the place where I grew up and holding the last little piece of my interrupted legacy like a torch he had been unknowingly passed. I hoped he didn't think it was his fault. He was never a part of this. He just so happened to cross my path right before the end.

He left at the perfect time, too. The cloud cover was just starting to break up right before sunset, creating holes in the sky where the warm amber sun could peek through. It created paintings of light across the ground that mingled with rolling dry leaves, discolored grass, and speckled stones. The way the sun hit the windows of the old train station made the place look alive, but only on one side. The other side was cast in cool shadow, glimpsing the reality of the building's lost glory. A sign on one of the upstairs windows appeared in my prized photograph of the day: "space for lease" written in faded red marker next to a spot of cracked glass.

I took as many photos as I could, trying to capture all of the colors at once. All of the shapes. For only a few minutes, the world was bathed in gold, and I felt the full responsibility of trying to catch it in my hands.

When the sky grew dark, I climbed up the steps at the front of the building, sitting with my back to the railing and my ass on cold, smooth cement. While I looked through the photos I had taken that day, I realized something that took the wind out of my sails before I even got to the editing room: my grandfather would have hated these. Every photo was devoid of life, focusing on the overgrown weeds and the chipped paint and the dirty, smudged glass. Even the impression of dusty handprints on the windows was a mere suggestion of its vibrant history, but it wasn't enough. It didn't feel real. It felt haunted.

"I guess I fucking failed at that too," I snapped at myself as I shoved my camera back in its bag. The sound of the hard plastic jamming up against the spare lenses made me wince, but I quickly pushed the bag far away from myself with my foot. This wasn't the ending that I wanted. My last, simple wish was for a *good end* – a send-off that I could be proud of. Even that was refused.

Against my better judgment, I checked my phone. It was after nine o'clock now, and the only text message waiting for me was a quick line from my aunt telling me that Grandpa refused to eat his dinner tonight. I looked at Megan's name again. It was a ritual now: every time I opened my phone, I'd stare at her for a few moments as if trying to memorize her. She was probably packing her things tonight. She was probably looking up cool places to visit in San Diego. She was probably in forums, asking for recommendations and making new friends who would happily show her around.

And I would never catch up.

I reached across the steps to grab my camera bag, pulling it toward me and zipping it up. When I did, I felt a cold wind on my face and heard a shiver on the train tracks, like the sound of stones rattling in a bag. Something was coming. The damp soil was trembling under the foundation of the building, so subtle that I couldn't feel it from the steps. Yet, I could see it from the way rings formed in the puddles that collected near the gutters.

Those few seconds of staring at the ground caught up to me. In moments, the train tracks were bathed in a blinding yellow light that pulled a startled gasp out of my lungs. My trembling breath formed a white fog in front of my face. The wind quickly took it away.

Blinking, peeking through my fingers, I watched as a massive shape pull up slowly, followed by the scent of diesel. It was a train, blacker than the sky beyond it and louder than thunder. When I stood, pressing myself back against the wall of the old station, I half-expected to see the homes across the way light up while neighbors hollered out their windows at the noise. No one even stepped out to look. The train slowed to a stop in front of me as a singular car came into view, sporting warm yellow lights and a chandelier inside. There were people in there. I could see the tops of their heads through the window, sitting calmly side-by-side or glancing to see where the train had stopped.

It appeared so quickly. I hadn't even noticed it until it was right in front of my face – a train so fast that the devil couldn't catch it.

I took a few tentative steps closer, as if waiting for permission. It felt right. Even if my brain wasn't sure, my feet were guiding me there. With my camera bag tight around my shoulders and every cell in my body urging me to keep moving forward, I grabbed the cold metal bar and boosted myself up onto the step with a grunt. Something about this felt like the only option. My mom had always told me that intuition would be my truest guide. And this intuition told me, deep down where no rational thoughts could reach, that this ride was meant for me.

A few of the passengers looked up from their books, their newspapers, or their conversations. An elderly lady gave me a soft smile while a young woman in blue scrubs moved a few inches to the side to give me a spot to sit. I took her up on the offer, sitting down next to her and coughing into my fist. The air was cold outside, but it was warm in the car. The old woman was wearing a light rose perfume that reminded me of my great aunt's house.

"Hey," the young woman said while tucking a book under her arm. "Sorry, it's a little crowded in here tonight."

"That's fine," I waved a dismissive hand. The young woman had pale skin, short blonde hair, and an arch in her brows that looked like guilt. Why did she think it was her fault? "Um … I-I didn't know passenger trains passed through her anymore."

"I didn't either," she said. "I'm not even sure where this one's going, if we're being honest with each other."

We shared an awkward chuckle during my last few seconds of hesitation. I almost thought about turning around and getting off the train, thinking of all the things I had left to do at home. I missed dinner. Grandpa needed his nighttime medication. But somewhere between fantasies of homework and doing the dishes, the train began to move. The choice was made for me.

"What are you reading?" I asked to break the silence. At that, the woman in blue scrubs pulled the book back out and tapped her fingers against the cover.

"It's, um, The Count of Monte Cristo," she said as she toyed with the worn cover. She spoke a little faster than she needed to, almost as if she worried her voice would take up too much space. "I-I thought it might be a long ride and … it's one of my favorites so–"

"You don't have to sell it to me," I teased. "I've heard it's great."

"One of the best," she nodded. Her timid posture seemed to calm with that tiny hint of approval, and I watched a small but genuine smile tug at the corners of her lips. She was pretty, I thought, but stress and exhaustion made her look older than she probably was. One of her feet began to tap, and I noticed the scuffed white shoes she wore. Paired with the uniform, I imagined this was probably the first time she had been off her feet in ages.

We both jumped when the train made a tight turn, the whistle muffled through the walls. One hand went to my chest, rubbing a sore, strained muscle.

"The first few minutes are always the roughest," a voice from the other side of the aisle said. I looked up to see a young black man smiling over a newspaper. He had small, round glasses and a blue denim jacket that was stained with oil, but his smile was warm and handsome. "You'll get used to it. Once this thing starts moving, it's the smoothest ride you'll ever have."

I adjusted my camera bag on my lap. "You a regular passenger?" I asked.

The man shook his head with the kind of soft, deep chuckle that felt like a heated blanket. "Nah, just been waiting to get a seat for a long time," he said. "My wife's waiting for me at the last stop. She's got our little girl with her. And – **whew**, boy, you would not believe how much I miss 'em both."

"I'm, uh ... I'm happy for you," I said softly, an unexpected lump forming in my throat. Something about the dreamy look in the man's eyes made me feel a deep, peaceful nostalgia that flipped my soul around inside of me. What did it feel like to be that happy? I cleared my throat. "So, where are we headed? I got on but never thought to ask."

The girl next to me let out a nervous, breathy laugh of relief, as if she had been too embarrassed to ask the same question. The old lady on her other side just hummed contentedly, but the man across from us kept reading his paper with that same cool-headed, pleasant smile.

"Fancy high-speed train like this? Who knows?" He voiced a deep belly laugh. "But, baby, I think we're gonna be just fine."

I didn't know why, but the way he said that was enough for me. *We're gonna be just fine.* I guess I didn't really need to know where the end was, so long as the trip there felt like home.

"You a photographer?" he asked, pointing at the bag. "That's one of those digital ones, isn't it? My pop used to have one of the old film cameras, but I tell you, every shot he took was blurry as could be."

I laughed along with him as I pulled the camera out of its bag, glad to see that the lens hadn't been damaged when I manhandled it. "Well, mine aren't much better," I explained. "I'm working on a college project right now, but it's not going so well."

"Ohh, complaining about it won't do you any good," he said as he folded the paper up and stuffed it against the seat behind him. Now, all of his attention was on me. "Come on, then, let me take a look."

While the man reached out a hand and curled his fingers at me, I hesitated for just a second before passing the camera over. He held it with surprising gentleness as he looked it over, trying to figure out how to turn it on. Eventually, I got up and wobbled over to his side to help him.

"There we go," he sighed as the gallery finally appeared. While I flipped through the photos, he adjusted his glasses with an intense, scrutinizing look. He thought deeply about each photo, and I watched his dark eyes travel over every pixel as if tracing the individual bricks like a true art critic. "These are very nice," he said. Not wonderful, not great, just nice.

"But they could be a lot better," I said. "I'm not sure what they need, but it's not what I wanted. I wanted something that would make my grandfather proud, but this–"

The man hummed thoughtfully with a nod of his head. "I see," he spoke softly, looking at another photo. This one paid extra attention to the chipped red paint on the front steps. "This station meant a lot to him?"

"This train, too," I told him. "He always told me stories about it. He said I would see it for myself one day – a sleek, black train that passed through in the middle of the night, moving so fast I'd miss it if I blinked."

"Glad you didn't blink this time," the man said with a friendly wink. I couldn't shake this sense that he knew so much more than I did, smiling pleasantly with his newspaper and the unsinkable confidence of a man who knew exactly where he was going.

I took a moment to gaze out the window, watching the landscape fly by. The sky was dotted with a million stars, and I could see the moon peeking out behind a light cluster of clouds. In the distance, I saw the glittering surface of Lake Erie. It was still and quiet, at that perfect time of year when the air was cool but the water was still warm from the late summer heat.

"The lake already?" I asked with a palm against the window. "There's no way we're this far north."

The young nurse next to me was looking wistfully into the

glittering water as if she hadn't seen it in years. In her eyes, I could see the reflection of so many childhood memories, camping trips, vacations, and sunburns. "It took us hours to get here when I was a kid," she said. "Are we really moving that fast or … did I fall asleep?"

"They built this train to move like lightning," the man across from us said with a fond smile on his face. "I always said it was so fast, the devil couldn't catch it if he tried."

And that time, he looked at me first. For just a second, I could imagine his dark brown eyes dotted with pale blue cataracts and the subtle moles and freckles on his cheeks intermingled with deep lines. But then that youthful twinkle came back, and he was looking out the window with the rest of us at the passing scenery. I was content to listen to the nurse next to me talk all about her parents' RV and how they would bring her and her older sister up to the state park three times a year. She went on and on, talking fast as if she had a limited amount of time, sometimes pausing to apologize for saying too much.

"We don't even talk anymore," she concluded with a tight, disappointed frown. "I guess my sister was always the glue that kept us together."

She was staring at an empty seat across the way, her eyes unfocused and blank. But behind them, I could almost see the flash of so many memories and years that she'd never get back. Her skin was chapped, and deep purple bags drooped below her eyes, but she couldn't have been more than five years older than me. She was still too young for an expression like this.

"My parents probably wish it was me," she said, unprompted. A moment later, she backpedaled as if she had said something wrong. "Sorry, it's not your problem. Sometimes this sort of thing just falls out of my mouth and I can't keep it all in, so I tell people things they don't even care about–"

"It's alright, it's fine," I said, interrupting her breathless rambling. My hands were up in a placating gesture, but I think it just made her feel worse. "It's cool. Let it out if you need to let it out; we're all friends here. Right?"

The man across the way nodded, his eyes closed and lips slightly pursed: serious, but holding back opinion.

The nurse, with her hands clasped in her lap and one leg bouncing in a quick rhythm, took a sharp breath in through her nose and avoided any eye contact. I watched the old woman on the other side of her discreetly slide a hand onto the young woman's knee, giving her the gentlest squeeze with wrinkled fingers. The nurse closed her eyes and let out a long, slow breath until her leg stopped shaking.

"I'm okay," she finally said. "Sorry."

"Don't apologize," I told her. "My family was never much for camping, you know. Must have been nice by the lake, right?"

And for the next hour, we all talked about *everything*. We talked as if we had all known one another for years. The old woman spoke, her voice a soft quiver that silenced the rest of us, and she told us stories of her childhood in Austria and how she met her husband, both of them young in a time of war. She had children, grandchildren, and great-grandchildren scattered all over the country now, and she remembered every single birthday and graduation. The man across the way, eyes shining with a wisdom beyond his years, told us all about his travels from one side of North America to the other. He talked a lot about his wife and how she loved to dance. I found myself hanging on every single word.

These were people with so much more life than I had, so much more experience. They were vibrant. I looked down the aisle, seeing other groups of strangers, all of them engaged in their own conversations. There were other worlds going on down there that we weren't even a part of.

It was at that point that the train started to slow. My fists clenched around the edge of my seat, breath catching in the softest gasp. "We're stopping?" I asked. I wasn't the only one looking around, silently asking for answers.

When I turned to look out the window, it was hard to see anything. Fog was rising from the ground, a dark blue cast over the softest suggestion of tall grass and distant buildings. And somewhere in the fog, I could see them: figures, standing together, waiting. There were so many of them.

Two seats down, the old woman smiled widely for the first time, a girlish joy in her rosy cheeks. "This is my stop," she said, a light in her pale blue eyes shimmering with excitement as a long-abandoned youth suddenly rushed back to her. I watched as she turned in her seat, waving at the figures through the window. And while I couldn't make out a single face in the crowd, she seemed to recognize each and every one of them.

The nurse stood up and offered the old lady her arm, which her wrinkled hands took gratefully. I watched the old lady give her the most tender look, stabilizing on her feet to reach up and pat the younger woman's cheek as if she were her own granddaughter. She brushed a knobby thumb over her dimpled smile, and the nurse leaned in to accept a kiss on the cheek, after which the old woman whispered something in her ear. I didn't hear what she said, but I saw the way the nurse's eyes opened a little wider, her expression far-off and thoughtful. Heartbroken, maybe.

The old lady toddled off, slowly walking toward the exit, where another stranger helped her down the steps. With an odd sense of grief welling up in my chest, I watched her step down and disappear into a swirling bank of pale blue fog. It swallowed her whole, but gently. Lovingly. And moments later, the train began to move again, those figures dipping back into the shadows together with one new member among them.

As the train picked up speed again, no one said anything. The man across from me had his hands clasped in his lap, leaning back to watch trees rush by through the windows. The nurse beside me was still looking at the floor. The silence that passed between us was peaceful, melancholic, and filled with unanswered questions.

"She whispered something to you," I said.

The nurse's eyes finally met mine. She gave me a nod and a slight smile, still visibly mulling over the words in her head. "She said, when my stop comes, it's okay to leave all the weight behind."

Despite not knowing one another's names, I felt like we both understood something about each other then. We weren't on that train for the same reason as that sweet old lady or the man across from us. The old woman went on to her destination with peace and calm, knowing what was waiting for her when her feet touched the ground. The man across from us had the confidence of someone who had been holding this ticket for years. The blonde woman and I? We both stepped into the train car because the thought of going home hurt more than this uncertainty. We didn't know where we'd end up. We both just wanted to leave.

But when I looked into the swirling fog as we cut through miles and miles of unfamiliar land, I was scared of what would be waiting for me when we reached my own destination. It worried me more than I thought it would.

Every time the train slowed to a stop, someone in the car perked up with a look of recognition. It was a little different every time. At one stop, we saw tall buildings and slow-moving traffic nearby, their headlights pale and ghostly. At another, we saw a long field full of sunflowers and distant storm clouds, heat lightning illuminating the blue horizon with color.

I could never make out the faces of the people waiting at the edge. At first, I thought it was simply the darkness that did it. In time, however, I figured I couldn't see them because they weren't meant for me.

After a long, quiet hour of traveling through a thick woodland, we were at a new coastline. Instead of storm clouds, this time I could see the slightest hint of a sunrise. It was just enough to paint a few fluffy clouds with a faint edge of pink and purple. As soon as it all came into view, I watched the nurse beside me perk up and turn around so that her whole body was facing the window, her hands on the glass like an eager child.

"I know this place," she said under her breath. "This is our camping spot. My big sister taught me how to swim."

The realization hit her slowly. I could see the thoughts forming in her mind through her eyes, plunging her into a deep and somber thought that was gradually replaced with peace. Acceptance, maybe. And for the first time since I had boarded, I watched her expression of worry and stress fade to a gentle, easy smile.

"This is my stop," she said.

The train began to slow. The nurse held the back of her chair in such a tight grip that she was shaking a little, but that eagerness in her eyes turned to relief and joy when a dark figure appeared at the edge of the train tracks. I couldn't make out the face, but I saw just a hint of long hair and an arm shoot up in an ecstatic wave.

The nurse waved back, tears in her eyes. "I have to go," she said, standing up before the train even stopped. "She's waiting for me. I..."

She paused, finally looking over at me and then the man across from us. I knew she was debating something then. Perhaps it was hesitation, perhaps it was guilt. The look of shame on her face told me that she thought she would be punished for this, but the peaceful smile from the man with the glasses seemed to put her at ease. *It's okay to leave all the weight behind.*

"I'll see you again someday, okay?" she said, now looking at me. Her bottom lip was shaking. We both knew it wasn't going to happen.

"Yeah," I said, surprised that I was choking up too. "Yeah, we will."

I almost asked her for her name, but I didn't. In the end, I think it was better that way. But before she had a chance to go, I found myself standing up and reaching out for her with urgent hands that couldn't bear to see her go without holding her just once. She didn't hesitate. She hugged me back so tightly – so *desperately* – that it felt like she had been waiting for that hug for years. She clutched the back of my shirt and pressed her head into my shoulder for a breath in time. I could feel her tears wetting the fabric.

And then, she let go. She had a huge smile on her face as she hurried down the aisle, jumping down the stairs two at a time with the kind of energy that turned her from a 25-year-old to a 10-year-old in less than a second. Watching through the window, I saw her rush clumsily into the mist until she collided head-on with the figure waiting for her. And for just a moment, I was let into her little world long enough to see her embracing a woman with blonde hair and a tan, just a few years older than she was. The nurse hugged her so enthusiastically that she lifted her off the ground, spinning her in circles while she cried in a kind of ecstatic joy I had never seen before.

I didn't notice that I had tears rolling down my cheeks until I felt them drip off my chin. Quickly, I wiped them, looking around to make sure no one saw.

She seemed so happy, I thought. Her choice to step off the train and leave everything behind was a gift to her. I realized then, even though I never knew that woman's name, that she must have been stronger than any of us to hold such unimaginable pain and still be so relentlessly kind.

The man across from me must have noticed the look on my face, because he spoke up a few moments later to distract me. "Hey," he said, leaning forward. "Mind showing me those photos again?"

I hadn't thought about the photos I took in hours. I was too distracted by the view, by everyone else's stories, by these other lives. But the mention of my photography project pulled me back to the present. Back to myself.

"Sure," I said, getting up from my seat to sit next to him instead. Sniffling a little, I prepared the camera so that he could scroll through the photographs again. This time, he looked at them with the same thoughtful eye, but he wore a more satisfied smile.

"I think I know what these photos need," he said. "You should try taking them again in the springtime. You see, the autumn leaves just don't add the kind of life you need here. I think you should come back once the wildflowers are in bloom and there's fresh green ivy everywhere. Then – oh man, it'll be real pretty."

He wasn't looking at the photos anymore, his eyes squarely fixed on mine with a sense of deep, knowing kindness. My heart ached when I realized what he was trying to do. What he wanted me to do.

"That's not a bad idea," I said, trying to picture the wildflowers in my head. "Thank you."

"Anytime," he told me. He gave me a gentle pat on the knee and handed the camera back. "My stop is coming up next. Why don't you step off with me? I'll make sure you get home safe."

I didn't question it. I didn't have time to, really. The train began to slow again, that soft sunrise appearing over the buildings and the trees, and I realized how familiar everything looked. I could see my school in the distance. We passed the mechanic shop where a few rusty cars had been parked for years. Finally, the train stopped right in front of a brick archway and a set of concrete steps. The train station.

"This is your stop?" I asked, my eyebrows squeezed close together.

"Sure is," the man said, a wide smile on his face. "My favorite place in the world with my favorite people in the world waitin' for me." I looked away from him long enough to see two figures approaching, walking down the concrete steps hand-in-hand. One was a woman and the other was a child with her hair in braids. Even though

I couldn't see their faces, I felt such a deep pain in my heart. I wanted them to be waiting for me instead. I wanted them to be *mine*.

"Go on ahead," the man in the glasses said, sensing my hesitation. "I'll be right behind you."

When I stood up, I spared him another glance, seeing the satisfied grin on his face and the way his eyes glittered with something akin to pride. In that moment, I had never trusted anyone more in my entire life.

"I'll see you around," I told him, choking up a little. And this time, I knew for a fact it wasn't true. That was okay. I was content with what we had. He and I got to have so much time together already.

Before I stepped onto the platform, I heard him one last time. "You're doing great, Billie-girl," he said. His voice sounded different now – older, softer, sadder. I didn't turn around to look at him. I wanted to remember him just as he was moments ago, smiling with all his teeth and staring at the red brick archways in awe while mist formed on the lenses of his little round glasses.

The moment my feet hit the ground, a gust of wind from behind scattered my hair in every direction. I didn't even need to look over my shoulder to know that the train was gone. It left no trace behind, no sound, no smoke. If the devil had been following it, he wouldn't even know which way it went.

The walk home was anything but quiet. For the first time, I didn't resign myself to a slow shuffle with my head hanging low. I paid attention to the morning birds in the trees, to the kids laughing and pestering each other at the bus stop, to the church bells a few streets down. That short time I spent on the Black Bullet made me aware of all the stories around me, intersecting with my own like galaxies drifting side-by-side. In every stone on the sidewalk, there was an entire history. In every person who nodded politely, there were generations of ancestors who all culminated into one singular smile. No one was a stranger anymore.

I opened the front door and took my shoes off by the kitchen, listening to the quiet tick of the clock. The lights were still off, but I saw sparkling dust particles in the sunlight that filtered through the dining room window. It seemed brighter than ever this time.

"Grandpa?" I asked, shrugging off my hoodie and tossing it over the back of a chair. "You won't believe what I saw on my walk last night."

He didn't answer. I stood at the kitchen sink, looking out the window at the mourning doves perched on the tree. The back of my throat tightened and I choked up again, gripping the basin hard with both hands. Instead of hoarse, throaty snoring from the next room, I heard peace.

"I can't wait to tell you all about it," I said out loud to a man who wasn't even there anymore.

But he already knew.

Saint Lily

The night before they found her, swamp gas bubbled up to the surface and ignited. It must have been something about the conditions in the air after the spring thaw, or maybe it was the storm clouds rolling in that made the fresh mossy ground light up in cold colors. There were no photos. No videos. But when morning came, four men from down the dirt road put on their long rubber boots to wade through the marsh, entertaining whispers of visitors from another world.

She must have been frozen, they said. She must have been there all winter. When her body rose to the surface, floating on her back with her eyes closed and black beetles crawling between her lips, Gregory Myers whispered the name of the holy mother and drew a cross over his heart. This was a miracle, they all agreed. She was no older than twenty-one, with long brown hair that fanned around her shoulders and tangled in the weeds. She was a vision, unclothed and impossibly clean, with unchipped polish on her fingernails.

And they called her Saint Lily, named after the flowers that were freshly blooming at the edge of the grave they plucked her from. Their petals disappeared against cold white skin as the four men carefully covered her in spare bedsheets and carried her down that long dirt road, all while passing drivers craned their necks to see a silent procession of waterlogged pallbearers. Droplets of holy water followed them.

A glass coffin was made for her – a vulnerable and voyeuristic display. Shirley, the pastor's wife, watched with a disgusted wrinkle above her nose while her husband laid out a clean white cloth for Lily's body to lie upon. "It's ghastly," she said. Moments later, when she was invited to see the body for herself, she resisted until she caught a glimpse of the woman's long, dark hair. Those untidy strands would not do.

"No," Shirley said as she pushed her husband's hands away from the preparation. "You're doing it all wrong. Get me a comb. We can't leave her hair a mess like this."

As she brushed a long-toothed comb through Lily's hair, she was gentle with her tangles and knots. She plucked the dried weeds and twigs with so much tenderness, it was as if she thought she was still alive. *Maybe she is*, she found herself thinking, before the lack of breath and the cold, stiff skin under her fingertips brought her back to her senses. All the while, she found herself speaking aloud, asking the question no one else had even entertained yet. "What happened to you, sweet girl?"

Pastor Vincent had his hands folded behind his back, standing near the wall. "We don't question God's miracles," he said in the smooth tone of a man well-versed in gentle scolding. And yet, the waver in every word revealed his own uncertainty.

Shirley shivered as she touched Lily's face and brushed away specks of dry leaf and marsh debris. She delicately pulled a small twig from the girl's mouth. That hint of a blackened tongue felt like icy fingers wrapping around the back of her neck, tangled in thin strands of graying hair. For the briefest of moments, she wanted to turn to her husband and berate him for being so callous. Maybe this girl had a family looking for her. What if she was missing? The police would surely want to know.

But a golden light hit the stained glass windows at just the perfect time, and Shirley no longer thought about police or coroners or grieving parents. Stormclouds parted and gifted them with stunning, prismatic colors that trailed across the chapel floor and turned Lily's coffin into a shimmering treasure. Hints of red and gold appeared in her hair, the paper color of her skin now glowing with angelic light: perfect, pure, and not of this earth.

"You're right," Shirley said breathlessly, her thin hands pressed against her heart as she backed away. "She was a gift."

It wasn't long before every sermon at the church included Lily's name, with offerings of marsh flowers laid below her and members of the congregation lining up to gaze upon her one at a time. They each had only a few seconds, and those who caught her when the sun was brightest often wept at her feet in ecstatic relief. *We're chosen*, they whispered. This small town, surrounded by woods and a web of empty dirt roads, must have been special. They were more worthy, more pure than other small towns and other dirt roads.

Jonah sat at the back of the church during the procession of offerings, his hands clasped together atop his knees as he pressed his forehead to the back of the pew. He was staring at the space between his shoes. Tonight, it was his turn to hold the vigil. Once the sun went down until the early hours of morning, he would sit in this chapel, alone with Lily. It was going to be a cloudy night – no stars, no moon. He would be alone in the dark with a corpse, tasked with some supernatural responsibility to make sure she didn't sit up and speak in tongues while no one was looking.

He didn't notice the weight that pressed down on the seat next to him until his friend, Michael, cleared his throat into his fist and began to bounce his leg with nervous energy.

"Tonight's your night, huh?" he asked, looking at Jonah from the side. "It'll feel like forever."

Jonah tore his eyes away from the polished hardwood floor to take in Michael's tired eyes and the fresh specks of gray in his hair. They went to school together, turning thirty-one that year, only a couple of months apart. Somehow, Michael looked about ten years older.

"What happened when you watched her?" Jonah asked.

Michael shook his head first, his eyes scanning the room: the stained glass, the high ceiling, the white walls that made it all look brighter. "Nothing much," he finally said. "She didn't get up and walk away if that's what you're worried about."

Jonah laughed. "I'm not saying she would–"

"But you'll feel like you're drowning," Michael continued. His eyes held a deadly seriousness, cold and direct. He barely blinked.

"The hours seemed longer, you know. And I-I've *done* a vigil before, remember when my Aunt Millie passed? This was different. Something was wrong. I felt ... judged, like she knew I was there and she was angry at me. Like she's angry at *all of us* for letting this happen to her, and we're gonna pay for it."

And while he spoke, an old woman at the front of the church began to wail. She fell to her knees, her forehead pressed to the glass of Lily's coffin, while her hands pressed all over its cloudy, fingerprint-stained surface. Jonah winced when he noticed the floral-printed scarf wrapped around her head. Mrs. Pierce had been battling cancer for months, but the glittering rays of sunlight that bathed her thin, delicate flesh made her feel cured. The devil put that tumor in her, she thought, and Saint Lily took it away.

Michael took in a sharp breath, voice trembling. "She whispered too," he said after a long pause. "The body. She moved and she talked. I watched her breathe, Jo."

"Probably gas ... you know, from the swamp," Jonah said quietly, tearing his eyes away from Mrs. Pierce. When he looked over at Michael, seeing his wide eyes and pale skin, he looked away quickly. "I've heard it builds up in the body and makes 'em look like they're moving around, makes 'em sigh and groan. It's natural."

Michael didn't respond. His leg was still bouncing, his hands shaking, his eyes darting from side to side as if waiting for some inevitable danger that only he could sense. Jonah sat patiently beside him, one thin tether that kept him rooted in reality. For the rest of the service, they sat there in silence and listened to the sounds of worship, sorrow, and reverence. Jonah felt like an island.

After church, Jonah didn't go straight home. While his truck bounced along the rough, unpaved road that led to the tiny house his father had helped him build, he saw the old man himself, dragging a chainsaw through his yard and toward the barn. Jonah slowed to a stop in the driveway, taking a moment to look up at the new coat of paint on his parents' farmhouse before he stepped out. His father stopped what he was doing, letting out a pained grunt. His sore back was acting up again.

"What's the chainsaw for?" Jonah asked, slamming the rusty door shut. "You should be resting, ya' old fart."

His father, a bony man named Rick with a shiny bald head, wiped some sweat from his face and left a dirt stain behind. "Got trees to trim," he answered. "That thunderstorm brought down that old dying oak, and I'm carvin' it up for firewood. Gonna have some good logs for the fireplace."

"The oak's gone?" Jonah asked, squinting and putting a hand over his brow to shield from the sun. "That's a damn shame."

"Sure is," Rick said with a heavy sigh. "You used to have a tree-house up there, remember that? Until that tornado brought it down … And the tire swing, too." That tree had been there for generations, showing up in the background of family photos that dated all the way back to when their ancestors first arrived from somewhere in Finland. But Rick's troubled expression was about more than the tree.

"You should have asked me to come by first," Jonah said with a sniff, the cold air getting to his sinuses. "I can take care of the tree for ya'."

"You're not doin' that," Rick said. He squinted into the distance, waving at Jonah's mother through the window. She didn't come out. "Besides, you're busy tonight. I heard you've got vigil. Gotta be well-rested for that sort of thing."

Jonah nodded quickly, hands in his pockets. "Yeah, I do. I'm heading back there around nine."

"Gonna be a long night," Rick said, clapping the dirt off his hands and then wiping them on the front of his jeans. He gave a weary, disapproving sigh. "I still don't know why they don't just put that poor girl in the ground."

"They're saying she's a miracle," Jonah explained. "You know, because she's so … well-preserved and whatnot."

"Probably the frozen marsh water," Rick said. His old eyes scanned the treeline where the woods met the yard, and he knew the swamp was beyond that. "She ain't from heaven, she's just a kid. Probably some out-of-towner."

He pulled a pack of cigarettes from his front pocket and offered one to Jonah, which he took. *Bad habit*, Rick always said, but he still offered his son a cigarette when they were talking about something stressful. If he was lighting up with him now, it meant there was far more on his mind.

"You look tense," Jonah said, taking a puff and watching it drift away in the wind. He watched his father's eyes dart from one thing to another: the rusted tractor, puddles in the dirt, the first buds of spring. The two of them had the same brown eyes, but the old man's looked less vibrant than usual.

"I was doin' some hunting back in November," Rick said after a long silence, coughing into his elbow.

Jonah let out a hoarse, sudden laugh. "That was out of nowhere," he said. "What about it?"

Rick didn't say anything for a bit. Instead, he was eyeing the forest again, a deep wrinkle between his gray, bushy eyebrows. "Just thinkin' about something I heard out there near the swamp, right before that big snowstorm. We must have had more foxes in the woods than we usually do." His voice was slow, soft, and careful, every word carrying a heavy weight. "When they cry at night, it sounds an awful lot like a woman screamin' bloody murder. It's pretty startling."

The two men shared a look: long, silent and grim. Jonah felt a sickness in the pit of his stomach, but he didn't linger on it. "It must have been foxes," he said simply, choosing to believe it was true.

He skipped dinner that night, feeding his cat but not himself. When he reached down to pet her long, black fur, she hissed at him for the first time since he found her six years earlier. She was usually so sweet, too. "Well, ain't you sassy," he teased, putting his shoes back on before leaving the house. He hadn't gotten any rest that afternoon; he knew he wouldn't. But his heart was beating too fast and his blood was too hot to let him feel tired.

He didn't ask to be nominated for this. He didn't want this, but he was far too proud to say 'no'. Jonah was made of tougher stuff, they always said, and he didn't argue. Even as a boy, everyone commented on his quiet nature and his no-nonsense attitude. They questioned the way he didn't play and goof around like other kids. He was unshakeable. But as he passed by Michael's house, seeing all the lights off and the curtains drawn shut, he felt the powerful urge to turn around and go home.

That temptation lingered, gnawing at him a little bit more with every stop sign and turn, until the headlights fell upon the dusty church road. The lights were on in the foyer where Pastor Vincent waited, close enough to see Jonah's truck through the window. That fact alone took away the burden of decision.

When Jonah arrived, he pulled his hat off before stepping through the front doors, noticing how different the place looked after dark. Those big, well-lit rooms and white painted walls seemed crowded now. Small, narrow, dull.

The pastor was sitting at the edge of the room, his elbows on his knees. A dirty yellow glow from the parking lot filtered through the window, leaving an orange cast against his shoulders. "Almost thought you weren't gonna show tonight," he said.

"Promised you, didn't I?" Jonah responded, hanging his hat and his denim jacket up on a nearby coat rack. He crinkled his nose a little. Without the overwhelming smell of rose and begonia perfume that usually followed the elderly church ladies, the chapel smelled like rotten eggs and swamp grass. "You look tired, Pastor. Why don't you head home and I'll take it from here?"

He could see the exhausted, lifeless weight in the older man's face, the way gravity seemed to be fighting harder to make his eyes droop. Pastor Vincent, as passionate as he had been about their town's miracle, seemed drained. Regretful. Questioning everything.

When he finally pushed off the bench and stood, Jonah had to hold his elbow to keep the pastor upright. The old man hobbled a little when he walked – he had never done that before. "I'll keep you in my prayers tonight," Vincent said after giving Jonah a soft pat on the shoulder. "Six o'clock. I'll be here to unlock the doors for you."

"I'll be waitin'." Jonah watched him go, noting the way the old man never looked back even once. No small talk. No pleasantries.

Being in that chapel had never felt so cold, so dark, so unlike itself. Jonah pushed in through the heavy double doors, finding the smell of swamp gas to be stronger the moment his feet stepped into the chapel proper. There were flowers left to rot on top of the coffin and petals on the floor. There was no moon to shine its light through the stained glass, leaving the room so dark that everything held an eerie outline as his eyes adjusted. He could see fuzzy specks of color in his vision, like white noise.

The body was there, that lily-white vision of purity and goodness. Using the flashlight on his phone, Jonah picked up a handful of long white candlesticks and placed them into each of the gold, tapered holders that surrounded the coffin. He lit them with a box of matches left behind.

The candlelight dancing on Lily's face didn't help the uncomfortable feeling. Jonah didn't want to stay. Instead, he found a spot at the back of the room, sitting down with his hands on his knees just as he had that morning when he was half-listening to the service and watching the procession of worshipers drop their offerings at Lily's feet.

All he had to do was sit and watch, he reminded himself. Sit and watch this woman rot away. Slowly. Mysteriously. Tragically.

The first hour was slow and static. Jonah picked at a spot of paint on his jeans, bringing back the memory of the shed he still hadn't finished working on. Between extra shifts at the gas station and that cold, brutal winter, his side-projects had mostly gone to hell. He wondered if Lily had left any unfinished business behind. She could have been a student. Maybe she had a date coming up that she never met, or a new job she never showed up for, or a good book she would never get to finish. She shouldn't have been here.

For the second hour, he spent time looking out the window, watching the corn fields sway in a light breeze. Heavy clouds were rolling overhead, bringing plenty of wind but no rain.

There came a time when the movement between the corn stalks became purposeful, however. Strange. Erratic. He squinted his eyes, expecting to see a wandering deer or someone's dog running off its leash. Maybe someone was out there, he thought. Maybe someone was skulking around in the dark, creeping outside the church, keeping secrets.

This little village was full of them. He knew that. No one ever talked about the boy who went missing fifteen years ago, the farmhouse fire that was started from the inside, or what they found in Mr. Garner's basement. It was better for Jonah not to ask, not to look, not to think unless he was prepared to carry those secrets with him for the rest of his life. That was the nasty thing about secrets. The very nature of them would always entrust somebody with responsibility they didn't ask for.

Something about the movement in the corn, the winds picking up, and the dark clouds overhead made Jonah tense. His eyes drifted up to the solitary street lamp in the church parking lot, shining a dirty yellow light over the pavement. It flickered often, he thought. This felt different.

When Jonah turned from the window, something in the room seemed different. He couldn't put his finger on it. He began to circle the pews, his calloused fingers grazing the edge of the wooden seats that had been worn down from years of oily hands and children's crayon drawings. One of them seemed a little crooked, as if it had been nudged. The pews at the front of the room, closest to the coffin, felt colder.

The coffin itself, Jonah noticed, was trying to draw his eyes in. He faced away from it, his back fully turned even though he knew it was disrespectful, but he still felt this nagging need to check Lily's body with his own two eyes. The rational side of him that took up ninety-nine percent of his brain knew that it was silly. Stupid. The other little sliver was already imagining visions of the coffin top sliding open on its own, the body inside sitting up, her eyes impossibly wide and pale while marsh water dribbled over her bottom lip.

The temptation got the better of him in time. He turned, glancing only out of the corner of his eye. He was embarrassed by his relief the moment he realized the corpse inside the glass coffin hadn't moved an inch. She was still there, still lying on her back, still as pale and stiff as ever. Calling her 'beautiful' put a weird taste in his mouth, but it was true. A dry, wilted petal from the bouquet sitting atop her coffin broke off from the stem, tumbling down to the floor.

He hadn't seen the body up close, he realized. He never really had a desire to. But now, as he found himself locked in a dark room with only candlelight to guide him, there was nothing to do but stare and wonder. There was nothing to do but think.

He heard the crunch of a dry petal underneath his boot when he stepped up to the coffin, looking down at Lily's face. His eyes avoided her body at first, out of equal parts respect and shame. But her face was entrancing enough. She had big, round eyes – he could tell by the hollows of her eyelids, the subtle wrinkles beneath them expressing sleeplessness instead of age. Her full, gray-colored lips had been tampered with already, marshland sludge and weeds pulled from between her teeth before they even put her in the coffin.

Jonah could understand why she was such a miracle. A wonder. If she had been his loved one, caked with makeup to mimic a flush of life before the day of her funeral, he might be fooled into thinking she was sleeping too. But there was no makeup. No paint. She was angelic all on her own.

That illusion was broken when he finally allowed himself a glimpse of her body, eyes scanning the expanse of dry, alabaster skin. She had bruises on her legs and her hips. Purple marks, small and close together, were flanked by a faded green hue that blended into the darker flush pooling at the spot where her flesh met the glass beneath her. It wasn't just blood sinking with gravity's pull. Someone grabbed her. Someone hurt her.

"What the hell is your story?" Jonah asked out loud, knowing Lily would never answer him. "You shouldn't be here."

There was no draft in the chapel, but the candles that flanked the coffin still trembled as if a light, cool breeze had drifted by slowly, touching them one at a time. Jonah picked one and stared into the flame, watching it grow fainter and then stronger. They'd burn out before the night was over. He'd have to change them soon.

How long did he stare into the flame? He only blinked when his eyes began to sting, growing dry and bleary. A challenge to see how much discomfort he could take. As soon as he closed his eyes for real, the sound of the church piano playing a single note made his breath catch and his shoulders jolt up with surprise. It was a mouse running across the keyboard, he was certain. Maybe a key had gotten stuck. They were old and finicky like that. A mind of their own.

In an instant, every candle around the coffin stood at attention, the flames burning bright and pointing at the ceiling as if all movement had been sucked out of the air. Even as Jonah walked by them, they didn't budge. It wasn't enough to get his imagination going, no – he was too rational a man to think like that. But it got his attention. He stepped away from the coffin, almost sensing that he had overstayed his welcome, and sat back down in the front pew with his hands clasped together atop his lap.

Jonah cast his eyes down at the floor. When the candles began to flicker naturally once more, he watched the way the shadows of his own hands danced around his ankles. He was transfixed by it, stuck in this dark and silent abyss where there was nothing else to capture his attention. This kind of quiet, uneasy boredom was the perfect recipe for making even the mundane seem extraordinary: the movement of clouds, the subtle odors in the air, the pattern of his own breathing.

He no longer heard any traffic on the main road. He didn't see flashing headlights against the window glass or the wave of corn stalks in the wind. All he saw was his own shadow, jittering so subtly it could have been his eyes playing tricks.

Jonah's shoulders grew heavier as time went on. His vision began to blur from exhaustion and boredom. He closed his eyes, knowing it was bad form, but allowing himself that moment of rest nonetheless. He wasn't a man of great faith. He knew this. He also knew that this vigil, which was holy only by name, was just a bastardization of actual religion created by backwoods cultists who only had a bare idea of the practice.

Even if he didn't go to church, he could at least agree that this congregation used to have dignity. It used to have a purpose. Now, they worshipped a corpse that should have been sent to an autopsy table and filled the chapel with rotten plants and the smell of bog water. *It doesn't matter if I fall asleep*, Jonah thought. *There's nothing holy about this.*

A split second before Jonah opened his eyes again, he heard a soft, dry whisper. It was so faint and so unintelligible that he couldn't figure out if it was real or part of a brief dream. His head shot up, his lungs taking in a sharp and sudden breath. His neck was stiff and sore from his drooping posture.

In that split second, while his eyes adjusted to a dark room, he swore he saw a second shadow looming over his own. It sank back before he even had a moment to ponder it. A trick of the eyes.

The first few sprinkles of rain were tapping against the windows, breaking an otherwise oppressive silence. Jonah's heart beat a little faster. He stood up on wobbly legs, still feeling half-asleep, and decided to pace back and forth to keep himself awake. And while he stretched his muscles and walked by the glass coffin, he noticed a slight change in Lily's position. No, not a change. It couldn't be a change. One of her elbows was bent, her hand resting on her hip as if subtly, modestly covering one of the bruises on her side. Jonah tried, but for the life of him, he could not remember where her hand had been positioned before. It was probably there all along, he thought. It must have been.

"I'm losing my goddamn mind in here," he murmured to himself, resuming his aimless pacing around the chapel. Maybe he would head to the kitchen and see if anyone had left a coffee maker. The scent of brewing coffee would be leagues better than the staleness in the air right now. He stepped away from the oppressive scent of swamp water and the cold chill trapped at the head of the room, instead standing near each of the windows in turn to watch the rain fall in an empty parking lot. Only, it wasn't empty for long.

Jonah watched a dark pickup truck pull in, obscured by the storm as a heavy wind picked up. The rain began to fall in sheets. At first, Jonah wouldn't have thought anything about the truck. That was before he saw two figures step out, one of them grabbing garbage bags and rope out of the back seat while the other carried a woodcutting axe.

He decided it was as good a time as any for a smoke break, thinking maybe he'd run into these visitors out back. As it happened, they moved faster than he did. By the time Jonah made his way out of the chapel and into the connecting back rooms where the church kitchen and offices were found, he already spotted wet shoe-prints on the floor and heard a pair of hushed voices.

"How are we doin' tonight, fellas?" he asked, flicking on the light in the kitchen. One of the men was scrounging around in a cabinet, the other pulling a ring of duct tape out of a drawer.

He recognized them both: Adam and Gabe. They were a couple of grades behind him in school, but Jonah wouldn't say they were friends of his. Now, over ten years later, one of them was a well-known methhead and the other had already served some time in jail for beating up an ex-girlfriend. They used to be good guys, once upon a time.

"We're relieving you of your vigil," Adam said, sniffing loudly and scratching the back of his neck. His skin was red and irritated and his fingernails were chewed down to bloody tips.

"Nah, you ain't," Jonah said, digging around for a cigarette before walking over to the exit, propping the door open with his boot. "Pastor and I had an agreement. I'm supposed to stay here until he comes to tap me out, and that's the plan."

"Yeah, well, plans are changing." This time, it was Gabe who spoke up. He seemed more mentally present than his friend, but more irritated as well. "Listen. Jonah, this ain't about you. Come on, man, just get the fuck out of here, okay? You're done for the night."

Jonah pushed a doorstop down, standing half-in and half-out of the rain to smoke his cigarette. He shook his head, brows knitted together with a heavy wrinkle between. "You must think I'm stupid," he said. "Now what in God's name – forgive me – are you doing here in the middle of the night with a fucking hatchet?"

Adam opened his mouth to speak first, teeth on his bottom lip as an expletive built up in his throat. It never came out, however, as a loud crash from the chapel made the three men jump. Thunder rumbled only a second later, causing the whole building to shiver under their feet.

"For fuck's sake..." Jonah tossed the cigarette into a puddle before rushing toward the chapel door. Adam and Gabe were a few steps behind him, abandoning their project long enough to get a look at the broken glass strewn across the floor.

Jonah's stomach did a flip when he noticed the largest stained glass window had been destroyed. It wasn't thunder that shook the building, he realized. The old oak tree had finally given out in the powerful wind, cracked in half by a bolt of lightning that left it still charred and smoking.

"God, no..." he murmured as he stepped around shards of glass. The massive branch, too big for one person to move, had some-how missed Lily's coffin by a few inches. It didn't matter. She wasn't in there anymore. The coffin was empty, the glass lid shoved to the side just enough to fit her body through.

Jonah turned to Adam and Gabe with an accusatory look of pure disgust. "Who else came with you?" he asked.

"No one!" Gabe held his hands up. "It's just Adam and I, we didn't do this–"

"Then who the fuck *took* her?" Jonah interrupted. "I don't know what the hell is wrong with the two of you or what you did, but you better come up with a good answer real quick." He was already reaching for his phone, about to call the police when Adam rushed forward to swipe at his hands.

"No!" he gasped out. "No, don't! Come on, man, we didn't do anything!"

"So you weren't bringing garbage bags and an axe in here to dismember a goddamn body?" Jonah shouted back. "You know something I don't."

Adam was pacing now, his hands on the back of his head. "It's a fucking corpse, man, they're keeping a corpse inside the church! It's fucked up!"

"It's devil worship," Gabe chimed in, the axe still perched on one shoulder as he tightened his grip on the handle. "Come on, Jo, don't tell me you believe all this bullshit about miracles and saint-hood. That abomination is straight from the devil."

"It's a woman's body," Jonah argued. "Not the devil, you dumbass. A real woman who died a real death. Now, I don't know jack shit about miracles or prophecy or all that, but what we're not gonna do is chop her up into pieces and get into even more trouble. Listen. We'll call someone tonight, we'll have the cops come take her away, but we're not doin' this right now."

"No. No cops." Adam was vehement. "We're gonna handle this alone."

"*We* are not doing shit," Jonah spat out. "I'm not helping you."

"But–" Gabe took a step toward Jonah, but stopped when the room suddenly went dark. The few candles that hadn't been extinguished by the wind finally tipped over, their flames sizzling out. The parking lot, once lit by a faint yellow glow from a single streetlamp, had gone black along with the entirety of the town.

"Shit!" Jonah hissed as he stomped his boot down on one of the candles, its wick still lit as it rolled toward his toes.

He didn't realize how dark the nights out here could get. His eyes adjusted slowly, but after a few moments of blinking away the swirling colors in his vision, he turned to see the faint outline of Gabe standing alone next to the empty coffin. "Where did your friend go?" he asked with an exasperated sigh.

Gabe was just as surprised as Jonah was, turning around and listening for the door. Maybe Adam got scared and ran. Maybe he rushed out when no one was watching. "Adam!" he yelled, a hand cupped over his mouth. "Adam! You dumb shit–"

While Gabe was yelling for his friend, Jonah was already turning on his phone's flashlight. As soon as the light pooled across the floor around his feet, he began to get his bearings: glass under his boots, leaves and splinters of wood scattered across the polished floor, and water dripping in from cracks in the roof.

He grimaced a little when he noticed the shape of wet, wrinkled footprints mixed in with the glass, leading from the chapel back to the kitchen. "Why did he take his shoes off?" Jonah asked. "Guy's out of his damned mind."

He followed the prints toward the kitchen, noticing a distinct spot where the water tracks stopped. Instead, a deep pool of fresh, warm blood took its place, collecting on the floor in a huge puddle that stretched in all directions with the grooves between the tiles. Jonah put a hand over his mouth as the smell hit him: metallic, strong, hot. Shaking, his fingers gripped the phone tighter as he followed the trail of blood, the puddles turning to streaks as if someone had crawled through it and left a snail trail behind.

"Holy shit," he whispered, gagging. There, leaning up against the counter, was Adam. He was sitting with both trembling hands up to his face, eyes wide and pupils small. His shirt was gray moments ago, but now it was stained red in a bib-like pattern that poured from his gaping mouth. It took Jonah a few moments to realize what was wrong: his lower jaw was gone. He didn't notice until he watched his tongue curling and flexing, almost as if searching for his bottom teeth.

Jonah fell back, sitting on the floor and pushing himself with his feet until he was pressed against the opposite wall. Gabe, who had been following behind at a safe distance, was throwing up in the sink. "What the fuck?" he cried between heaves. "Man, what the *fuck*? Oh my God. Adam, Jesus Christ, oh my G–"

"Shut up," Jonah said in a hoarse whisper, sweat trickling down his brow. His face was white and clammy, as if feverish. He had torn his eyes away from Adam's traumatized face, and they had fallen on his feet instead. His shoes were still on.

"There's someone else in here," Jonah whispered again, turning his flashlight over to Gabe. "We'll call for help when we get to the car."

Gabe was panicking, tears pouring down his cheeks. His legs buckled as he tried to stay upright. He looked over at Adam, seeing his silhouette writhing and struggling to move in the dark. "Man, he's still alive," he sobbed. "He's still fucking alive, bro–"

"I know," Jonah said, forcing himself back up to his feet. "I know, I know, I know…"

He was fighting to catch his breath, staggering over to the heavy back door. It had since been shut, the doorstop he had used only minutes ago now kicked across the room underneath a table. Immediately, he went for the doorknob and gave it a violent shake. It turned, but even his full weight couldn't get the door open.

"It's locked from the outside," he said.

"Bullshit," Gabe snapped back, nudging Jonah aside to check for himself. "You can't just lock it from the outside, that's not how it works."

Jonah lifted his arms and slapped them back down to his sides in exasperation. "Well, then, something is pushed in front of it. I-I don't know, man, I don't get it!" He was still trying to stay calm, to stay quiet. It was a losing battle when Gabe was smacking his full weight against the door, one powerful shoulder-check at a time.

"Fuck this," Jonah said, stomping across the room. "I'm going out the front."

He carefully avoided the puddle of blood as best he could while reaching for the axe that Adam had left behind. He picked it up, the handle still warm, and held it tightly in one fist. With that, he left Gabe to struggle with the back door while he headed back into the chapel, his flashlight pointed squarely in front of him. He didn't want to look up, to shine a light on the entire room and see what it had become. There was a dread settled in his heart that he didn't have a name or reason for, but it told him that the chapel wasn't empty. It wasn't safe.

He stopped for a moment, listening. He heard Adam's blood-choked wheeze and the rhythmic thump of Gabe slamming his body into the door. He heard the drip of water from the broken windows. Below all those sounds, somewhere at the other side of the room near the foyer, he heard a new sound: the slow, uneven wet smack of bare feet against the floor.

Jonah turned his light off, crouching down behind the closest pew. The crunch of glass under his feet caught the staggering figure's attention. A hoarse, feminine voice let out a gasp of air – not a startled sound, but an aggressive one, like air being sucked in through gritted teeth. It was followed by a wet cough and the slimy thump of something splattering onto the floor. Jonah covered his mouth to silence his heavy breaths.

Those uneven steps got a little faster, a little closer. Jonah sank lower to the floor until he was underneath the seat, moving slowly to avoid the scrape of glass against hardwood planks. He could only see a silhouette in the pitch black room. An occasional flash of lightning crept in through the windows and lit up his view, but never long enough for his eyes to truly adjust. In those moments, he saw pure white skin and dark hair. No shoes. No clothes.

There's no way, Jonah repeated in his mind over and over. *She was dead, she was cold, she was...*

Lily let out another wheeze, walking stiffly like an infant just learning how to use her legs. The way she leaned from one side to the other, her knees frozen in place, made the loose weight of her upper body and her limbs even more unnerving. Her head, usually limp to one side, would jolt up when she made a sound. It made Jonah think of an animal sniffing the air.

Gabe's cussing and shouting at the door got Lily's attention. She inhaled sharply, her voice like a bark, as she turned and interrupted her mindless pacing of the chapel. Jonah could hear the way she breathed, slow and rattling at first, then quicker as her attention snapped to the kitchen. The wet slap of her feet against the floor grew louder as she crossed the room with single-minded dedication. This was rage. This was pure, murderous fury.

Jonah held his breath as she passed, her body bringing a bitter chill and a horrid smell with it. Lightning struck nearby, a loud boom shaking the church, and a flash of white pulling Jonah's eyes back to Lily as she shambled. Despite her clumsiness, she had crossed the room in seconds.

When she was gone, Jonah closed his eyes and took a deep, slow breath. It would only take him a few seconds to get across the room and to the front door. If it was locked, he would break a window with the axe. If that creature got to him first, he would defend himself. The plan was in his head, so clear and so possible, and still he hesitated.

Finally, when he heard Gabe let out a scream of terror from the kitchen, Jonah forced himself to move. He slid out from under the pew, grimacing when he heard the shift and scrape of broken glass underneath him. The shards sliced into his hands and his elbows, making him grit his teeth. Lily would have heard that. He turned his light back on so that he could see the path in front of him, the floor covered in water and sludge that smelled like the bottom of a drainage ditch.

His boots slid and squeaked against the damp floor, but he caught himself on the arch between rooms. When the door was within reach, Jonah practically threw himself against it, letting his full weight hit the surface. It didn't budge. He put down the axe and used that free hand to fumble with the doorknob. His phone slipped and clattered onto the floor, and that was when he noticed the locks in place. Both of his hands were trembling while he tried to get a solid grip. His blood stained everything that he touched.

"Fuck," he swore under his breath, trying the doorknob again. It wouldn't move. "Come on, come on…"

Desperation led him to grab the axe immediately, taking a tight grip on the handle and swinging it toward the doorknob. If it was jammed, he'd take the whole thing off. The axe split the wooden surface with a loud crack, missing the locks by just an inch, and Jonah was quick to put a foot against the door and give a powerful tug. He misjudged the amount of rust that had gathered on the head of the axe, because the brittle thing broke apart in two pieces as soon as he swung it back a second time. It clattered against the floor when it flew out of his hands, skidding across polished wood. *Fuck.*

He was about to give up on the door entirely when he heard that hoarse, throaty gasp from across the room. Wet feet padded against the chapel floor, echoing in the large, silent space. And then, they stopped. Lily was breathing heavily, making a damp hiss between gritted teeth. Jonah froze as he felt her gaze fall upon him, the distance seeming smaller now.

Jonah slowly knelt down, listening for the sound of Lily's

feet. He heard nothing. He reached for his phone, his fingers wrapping around it. He thought, just for a moment, maybe if he was quiet enough, he could sit in the dark and she wouldn't find him.

His shaky, bloodied fingers fumbled with the buttons, trying to turn the light off. He managed after a few seconds, holding it tight against his chest as he pressed himself close to the door and tried to stay flat. Still. Silent.

Lily didn't move forward. She didn't move away. If Jonah squinted his eyes in the darkness, he could still make out the subtle hint of her silhouette, swaying and shaking her stiff shoulders at the other end of the chapel. He couldn't see her eyes, but he knew they were fixed on him, watching and waiting for him to move.

And yet, even as he sat completely still, Lily took the first step. Her bare foot slapped against the wooden floor and the glass shifted beneath her, crunching and scraping. The sound it made, painful and sharp, was enough to clench Jonah's teeth. All the while, she was trying to speak, but her lips would only move so much. The grunts and groans she voiced were so alien and unusual, Jonah couldn't tell if they were sounds of rage or a desperate plea for help. One of her hands was outstretched. Her stiff fingers cracked with every twitch, and she grunted whenever she stumbled into one of the pews, frustrated with the limitations of her own body.

Jonah still couldn't move. He wanted to. There was a wooden bench just a few feet away from him. If he could pick it up and hoist it over his shoulders, he could throw it through the nearest window and climb out in just a matter of seconds. He had to try. It took all of his willpower to shift his body and lunge for the bench, but he got there on hands and knees while the sound of Lily's struggling breath and angry sobs echoed through the church.

Jonah grunted as he tugged at the legs of the bench. It didn't budge. His heart sank, the reaction immediate and deep, when he realized the feet had been bolted to the floor.

He had never felt his emotions shift so quickly before in his life. Adrenaline and fear had turned to hope for only a second, then dropped back down to despair. His bloodied hands still gripped the edge of the bench as he heard those slow, uneven footsteps getting closer. She didn't run. She didn't pursue. She walked toward him with patience, savoring every last second until the smell of dead flesh and marsh water surrounded Jonah like an impenetrable fog.

She stood in silence, looming over his hunched body. Jonah had his eyes clenched tightly, his mouth in a straight line as if stillness would protect him. And while he held his breath, Lily's face was lit up by sharp flashes of lightning. Her pale, empty gaze had found the discarded pieces of the axe once meant to dismember her. To destroy her. And as she began to creep closer, the wheeze in her throat sounding more like a pitiful whine, Jonah could swear he saw tears of betrayal gathering in the corners of her eyes.

Lily's pale lips parted with a wet sound, followed by another sharp gasp of air. The noise made Jonah jump.

A clean-up crew had already started clearing away the debris by the time morning came. The church was one of their first priorities. It wasn't long before the village began to buzz, whispers and prayers and cries in the sunlight celebrating a new demonstration of *her* glory. Lily had performed her greatest miracle yet.

Pastor Vincent entered the chapel while volunteers were covering the bodies, mops and buckets of red-stained water scattered across the kitchen. The smell inside the church was almost unbearable. The old man shook his head in shame, regretting that Jonah didn't make it through the storm. And yet, to die protecting the saint was an end any member of their congregation would surely give anything for.

The pastor knelt down, looking at Jonah's wide, sightless eyes and the awkward angle of his neck. The tree must have hit him when it crashed through the ceiling, he thought. The impact must have been at just the perfect spot. But compared to the other two, his body was immaculately clean and pure.

"We'll build a tomb for him," he said to one of the volunteers. "A stone one with his name engraved, placed on that little hill in the graveyard. We'll plant lilies around it when springtime comes."

"And the two who broke in?" the younger man asked, wiping sweat from his brow. Like everyone who had showed up that morning, he looked sick to his stomach.

Pastor Vincent pulled the sheet over Jonah's face again, giving him some privacy in death. "We'll burn them," he said without hesitation. "It'll be a warning. I think it's what she would have wanted."

He stood up slowly, his knees crunching as he did. His old eyes fell upon the glass coffin, where Lily was lying peacefully inside. Her lips were slightly parted, her eyes closed in mimicked sleep. One of her hands was perched on her heart, a modest and delicate pose that distracted from the glass still embedded in the bottoms of her feet.

Wide Open Spaces

Staring into a blank white space for hours on end had become an ordinary part of my process. It was a delicate system, you see. The music had to be just right, filling my studio with an atmosphere that would transport me from one world to another. The lights had to be down. My tea had to be the perfect temperature. The canvas? Just the right size.

Nothing else mattered, nothing else existed, except for me and that empty white space.

It had been harder than ever to find that perfect process. Part of that could be blamed on my racing mind, sure. Another part of that could be blamed on the sleep I didn't get anymore. As I stared at the blank canvas, trying to imagine what would take up that space, my eyes always wandered to the window facing the vast, golden cornfields. In the morning, it was blanketed in the softest light and a gentle breeze made it move in waves and patterns that I could see from the second floor of my home.

At night, it was a vast sea of noise – shifting stalks, chirping crickets, the rustle of wildlife. But sometimes, all the sound would stop and the field would stand completely still. Those were the hours of night when I would close the curtains to keep away the constant, nagging feeling of being watched.

It had been a few weeks since I had slept through the night; since *something* started waking me up.

It was well after noon and I was still staring at the canvas, but that concentration was swiftly broken by a playful, rhythmic knock on my front door. I jumped, dropping my pencil with a few whispered expletives.

When I didn't get to the door fast enough, my visitor knocked a second time. "I hear you!" I said, my voice cracking awkwardly with my very first words of the day. I undid the deadbolt, then the lock before cracking open the door to find my neighbor standing outside in the sun with a box under one arm and the other shielding his eyes.

"'Sup," he said, making a clicking sound with his tongue and teeth. Adrian, the grungy 20-something who lived next door, was a self-described 'burnout' who had been floating between delivery jobs for the past year. "I got your order. No need to tip me – getting to lure my dark mistress from her solitude is enough of an honor."

"You need to stop calling me that," I said with a dry laugh, reaching for my wallet on the nearby secretary desk. My nose burned pink with embarrassment. "I'm tipping you anyway. I know those ten steps from house to house are just *agonizing* for you."

"The pain is unbearable." Adrian accepted and pocketed the money with practiced nonchalance. He knew he'd get a tip even if he refused. "Can I come in and put these down?"

"Knock yourself out," I said, stepping away from the door so that he could enter. He put the box down on the kitchen table so that I could begin separating the perishables from the pantry items. While I did, he put his hands behind his back and ran his eyes over the dining room walls, taking in each pinned insect, ghostly Victorian photograph, and piece of unsettling art.

"This one's new," he said, walking up to a large canvas. He recognized the signature at the bottom right: W for Willow. "Your latest?"

I finished putting the fresh fruit away and joined him in the dining room, arms crossed as I stood a few feet away. Adrian didn't look like he belonged there, the gallery on my walls contrasting with his threadbare hoodie, slouched posture, and the way his ash brown hair fell in his face. He was staring up at a portrait of a seated medieval woman, her pale, round face distorted and smeared in large spots of texture that popped off the surface.

"Yeah, just finished it last week," I told him. "Took forever to dry."

"I'll bet," he nodded, looking over his shoulder with a shitty smile. "Inspired by Francis Bacon?"

I gave him a nod, impressed that he remembered. I had told Adrian about some of my favorite artists months ago, and every now and again, he surprised me by bringing it up again. "It was like... a mix between Francis Bacon and some meat I forgot in the back of the fridge."

"That's so hot," Adrian said without missing a beat, coaxing a snort from the back of my throat.

Usually, I tried not to entertain his worst jokes with even a courtesy laugh. This time, it caught me off guard.

"Thanks for the groceries, by the way," I said. "I don't always have trouble going to the store by myself, but every now and then, I go through these phases–"

Adrian was already shaking his head and putting up a dismissive hand to silence me. "You aren't on trial, babe," he said. "I already know. And besides, I won't complain about getting more work." He gave me a playful nudge with his shoulder. It was a gesture I wouldn't allow from most. I watched him shove his hands into his worn, dirty jeans and turn around, trudging toward the door with a roll of his shoulders.

"Welp," he sighed. "I should get goin'. Long drive home, you know."

I scoffed, wearing a half-smile. "Dumbass." I followed him to the door, a small pang of anxiety welling up when I realized it was unlocked. *It's fine. We're standing right here. Nothing will happen if we're standing right here in the middle of the day.*

"Don't work too hard, okay?" Adrian said, breaking me out of that spell. Then, he snapped his fingers as a thought came to mind. "Oh! October, right? The gallery?"

I let out a long, shaky breath. Fuck, I forgot about that. I had agreed to do that stupid show months ago without even thinking. "Uh, yeah, yeah," I said. "It's, um, just a small show. Somethin' for the Halloween season."

"Thatta girl," Adrian wore a big grin, endearingly crooked

teeth on display. He deliberated for a moment, looking down at the floor and then up at me again. "I'll chaperone you, how's that? You can tell people I'm your assistant or something. Famous artists have assistants, right?"

I knew what he was trying to do. He could see the hesitation in my eyes, deep and dark and begging for a reason not to go to this event. And yet, he had put it upon himself to be proud of my career even if I couldn't muster the strength to do so myself.

"I'll think about it," I told him. "Now get outta here. You're breaking my concentration."

He stepped backwards through the door, pointing at me playfully as he went. "I will not apologize and I will do it again." He winked. "Later, crypt keeper."

"Later, freak," I said, leaning up against the door. I watched Adrian go for only a moment, observing his lazy posture and the way he stuffed his hands deep into his pockets as he went. But the moment his feet reached the sidewalk, my door was closed. The locks were back in place.

Adrian didn't realize it, but his visit had inspired me somewhat. As I headed back into my home studio, faced yet again with an empty white canvas, I noticed the open curtains and the view of the cornfield from the largest window in the house. During Adrian's visit, the afternoon sun had dipped to just above the horizon now, bathing everything in an orange light that reminded me of a wildfire. Maybe that was what I needed – to take that golden view and turn it red.

The subject of the painting alone wasn't what made it eerie. As I began to paint the large open sky, the cloudless sunset, and the endless rows of corn, the purposeful absence of any end made my skin crawl just looking at it. Wide open spaces had always made me uncomfortable. If there was no road, no building, no landmarks to keep your eyes locked onto, one could easily imagine that it went on forever. That was the inspiration here: an endless field, bathed in red and orange, with no destination to cling to.

It was different from my usual work. It was devoid of distorted faces or gnashing teeth, but somehow, it made me more uncomfortable than anything else I had ever made. I could only hope it found the right audience.

Working late into the night was no stranger to me. Even when the sun was far beyond the fields and the night sky was full of stars, the lights in my studio stayed on. I imagined this was a common sight for my neighbors: that strange young woman who never left her house, awake and walking the halls until the wee hours of the morning.

Not all of that time was spent painting. Near midnight, I had my coffee by the window at the end of the upstairs hall, looking out over the dimly-lit street. I watched the lights go out one by one in each of the houses. Adrian's stayed on for a while. I saw him shuffle out to his porch, lighting up a joint to relax before he inevitably went back inside to sleep. Whenever he sat there on his front steps, I remembered his many invitations to join him. I always said 'no', but I wouldn't deny that the temptation was there.

Even I had to sleep eventually. Near three o'clock, I closed up my studio for the last time and did one final check on all the windows and the doors. My home was like a fortress at night, every room closed up and every exit locked as if my house were a submarine. It was the only way I could rest, the only way I could satisfy whatever was fundamentally wrong with me.

It was never enough.

I lay in bed for an hour after that, staring into each of the dark corners of my room. The floorboards would creak and the walls would settle. It was an old house, yes. I knew that. This was something new.

My eyes stayed open as long as they could.

When morning came, there was comfort in seeing everything the way I had left it the night before. I shuffled out of my bed, my face slightly puffy and hair tangled. The blonde roots were coming in through the artificial black. I wrote a brief note in my phone, adding hair dye to the list of things I would ask Adrian for the next time he did my shopping.

My morning, which started at approximately ten o'clock, continued the way I always liked it. I made a bagel with peanut butter, put my morning coffee in a huge tumbler that would stay warm for hours, and went back upstairs to my studio. But as I was lacing my apron around my waist and pushing up my sleeves, I realized that not everything was as I had left it.

One thing was out of place that morning. Just one. The paintbrush I had used the night before, rinsed and placed neatly back into the cloth pouch with the others, was now sitting crossed over the palette. It was still a little wet.

"What...?" I whispered under my breath, picking up the brush and turning it over between my fingers. This slight change was enough to make alarm bells go off in my mind, but it was more than just that. When I looked at the painting I had started the night before, something about it was different. The change was so small, so subtle, but it was obvious to eyes that had stared at this canvas for hours. An addition had been added to the image. Between the rows of corn, a shadow was painted. It was such a thin spot on the canvas that most people would never even notice, but I noticed it. I hadn't done that. I hadn't decided on that.

I put the brush down, trying to calm my shaking hands. My first instinct was to pick up my phone and call the police, but I had been through that song and dance before. They never found anything. *It was the wind, Miss Bohmann. It was mice. You might have termites. There was a raccoon in the attic.*

Instead, I took measured breaths and placed my coffee cup on the nearby desk, wearing a mask of calm as if something could still be watching me.

My eyes traveled to the window, looking out over that dreadfully open space yet again. Between the stalks of corn, I almost expected to see something. Anything at all. Nothing was there except for the rustle of the husks and long grass blowing softly in a gentle wind.

Nothing else in my home was amiss. The front door was still locked from the inside, nothing had been moved, nothing had been touched. And yet, even as I got to work trying to undo that black stain on the canvas, I felt eyes on me – the vague, uncomfortable inkling that my own safe place had now been put under surveillance.

And when it came to locking that out, I didn't even know where to start.

In the late afternoon, Adrian brought over a small order from the corner store. It all fit in one bag, which he deposited lazily onto the dining room table as he entered my home. "Sent me to the store for two things, huh?" he teased. "You know, if you wanted to see me, you could have just invited me over."

"It's not about that," I said, slipping past him to lock the door the second I heard it close. From behind me, Adrian shuffled a little from foot to foot, biting back a dry chuckle.

"Trapping me in?"

"No." When I spoke, it was sharp. The playful energy that Adrian was attempting to build deflated in an instant and he stuffed his hands in his pockets, smile disappearing.

"Hey, come on, what's going on? Willow…" His voice was low and careful. He only ever called me by my name when he was serious – no stupid nicknames, no 'mistress' or 'crypt keeper' or 'vampire bitch'. And when the smirk was gone and the mischievous glimmer in his eyes had faded, he suddenly seemed more tired than usual. Maybe he hadn't been sleeping well either.

I hesitated. What I really wanted to say was *'I think someone or something is in my house'*, but those words caught in my throat before they could come out. Instead, I nodded my head toward the staircase.

"I wanna show you what I've been working on," I told him. "I could use another pair of eyes."

No one but me had ever been in my studio before. Until today, it had been my one truly private space where only me and my work existed. So when Adrian entered the room, he took a moment to look around at everything with a smile of interest and wide, curious eyes.

"Damn, so this is where the magic happens," he said, waiting until I waved him in to properly enter. He was careful of where he stepped, taking note of the plastic on the floor and several paintings that were drying after being glossed.

"Yeah, well, not much magic has been happening here lately," I said with a low sigh, stopping in front of my current canvas. "This one's been giving me trouble. I stared at it for days before the image started to come together, but I'm still having second thoughts."

Adrian stood behind me, his head over my shoulder. When I turned my head, he was squinting at the image with his brows lowered in thought. He was uncomfortably close, but I didn't move. He smelled like pot smoke and toothpaste, his shaggy hair tickling my shoulder.

"Does it make you uncomfortable?" I asked. "The painting..."

He was still thinking, and I could see his eyes dragging over every inch of the canvas with real examination. "A little," he said. "I'm still looking for it, though."

"It?" I asked.

Adrian wore a little smirk in the corner of his lips. "Yeah, like, the hidden face," he said. "Or whatever you put in here. You hid it really well this time."

"Ah," I hummed. Fuck, that was what I was afraid of. "I see. There isn't a hidden face, actually. It's just... exactly what it looks like. A big, endless, open space. I was hoping maybe you'd see the vision."

Suddenly, Adrian started to backtrack, his eyes no longer traveling over the image as he crossed his arms in front of his chest. "Oh, no, for sure," he said. "Now that you mention it, the whole thing does seem kinda' eerie. Like, at any point, something could jump out at you. You might not be alone."

"You're just saying that because it's what I want to hear," I said, feeling a pang of disappointment. It wasn't Adrian's fault. Suddenly, I was painfully aware that perhaps the intentions I had for this work didn't measure up to what was usually expected of me. "Maybe it would be better if I just stuck to what I usually do."

Adrian scoffed, and I felt a firm hand curl around my shoulder. "Don't be dramatic," he said with a dry chuckle. "You've already put a lot of time into it. Maybe it just needs a little something, like... I don't know, a hidden detail or a pair of glowing eyes or–"

"A shadow?" I offered, thinking back on the stain I had found that morning. I had painted over it now, sure, but I could still tell exactly where it used to be.

Adrian nodded his head, wearing a thoughtful smile. "Yeah, that would work," he said. "I'm kinda shocked you haven't done that already."

That simple statement felt like a revelation. "Maybe I did," I said, whispering it mostly to myself. *Maybe I did.* "Hey, uh... this is gonna sound really stupid, but do you think I sleepwalk? I mean, have you noticed anything?"

"Aside from your lights on in the middle of the night?" Adrian asked with a knowing smirk. "I guess it's possible. You know, I hear your music sometimes when it's hot out and the windows are open. Not that I'm complaining or anything, I like Joy Division just as much as anyone else–"

I laughed through my nose with a little snort. Suddenly, I was relieved. If I crept into my studio at four o'clock in the morning, it would explain everything. No break-in, no mysterious visitors, no one living in the walls. It was just me, drinking too much coffee in the evening and not getting enough sleep.

"So you admit it," I teased. "You do spy on me through the windows."

Adrian shrugged, playing along. "Only a little," he said. "You know, nothing serious, just the occasional peek to see if you're changing or getting in the shower."

"Shut the fuck up," I laughed. "You're disgusting."

Adrian gave my shoulder a little shake, still keeping his tone lighthearted. "At least I'm honest," he said. "Usually stalkers won't tell you they're watching you. So, really, you should be saying 'thank you' for how considerate and respectful I'm being right now."

"Oh my god," I let out an exasperated breath. "Get out of my house."

For all of his perverted teasing and lack of tact, I could tell what Adrian was trying to do. He knew something was making me uncomfortable. We had known each other long enough for him to understand why I was the way that I was, and how to defuse the growing anxiety that threatened to drive me even further into my solitude. Whenever that paranoia crept in again, he seemed to know just what to say to bring my logical mind back to the forefront. It kept me away from the urge to demolish every ounce of freedom and courage I still had left.

"Alright, alright, I'm leaving," he put his hands up in surrender as he started toward the door. I followed him into the hallway, closing up the studio behind him. He gestured for me to go down the stairs first. "By the way, I like the new piece. I'm not sure if that came through in my critique, but the colors are - *mwah*!" He made a chef's kiss with his fingers as we reached the dining room.

"It needs work," I said with a shrug. "It's not perfect yet. It's far from it, but–"

"*Ah ah ah*, stop right there," Adrian waved a finger in my face. "Take a compliment. Being self-conscious about your work – which is most people's dream, by the way – isn't very confident or sexy of you." The teasing smirk slowly turned into something more genuine. "You're doing great. You need to go easy on yourself, and you need actual sleep and three square meals a day."

"Sure thing, mom," I said through a badly hidden smile.

"I'm serious," Adrian dropped his voice a little. The way he looked down at me, eyes scanning over my face with a deadly seriousness, made me suddenly more aware of how heavy I was breathing. He smiled widely. "Don't tell me I'm gonna have to keep a closer eye on those windows just to make sure you're taking care of yourself. Because I will."

He leaned a little closer when he said that. I could faintly smell the smoke on his lips. If I wanted to, I could have counted the hairs on his scruffy chin or inspected every line in that shitty, crooked smile he always wore. He was missing a canine tooth, I noticed. It didn't bother me. If anything, every imperfection and blemish on his skin was a unique, purposeful stroke of artistic detail that made his face unlike other faces. It made me wonder if he stared at my imperfections, too.

"I'll keep the blinds open for you then," I said, only half-joking.

Adrian smiled a little wider at that, and I noticed the way his eyes flicked down to my lips for just a second. This rat bastard knew what he was doing, because a moment later, he pulled away and shoved his hands into his hoodie with an air of pride. "I'll be checkin' in," he said. "Anyway, I got deliveries to run. Have a good day at work, pretty lady."

He stepped off the porch, walking backwards and almost stumbling down a step he had forgotten about. He recovered by the time his feet hit the sidewalk, murmuring something about 'meaning to do that'. It wasn't until I began to close the door that he turned his eyes away from me, but I could still see that spring in his step through the window. He was awfully pleased with himself.

I rubbed between my eyes, feeling a headache coming on. I didn't have time for this. For *him*. I needed to work, I needed to sleep, I needed to figure out what the hell I was going to do with this gallery showing in October. No matter what I did, I felt like the work was never done. It was never perfect. Complete.

It felt stupid to go back to my canvas and paint the shadow back in. And yet, when I got back to the studio and took a long look at the image, I knew that it was the right decision. The empty, open landscape just wasn't enough. It didn't fit. Alongside the rest of my work, riddled with distorted faces and horrifying images of things that crawled out of nightmares, this landscape looked as if it had been made by someone else. I couldn't have that.

My sleeping mind must have known better, I told myself. Late into the afternoon, I added the shadow back in, carefully detailing every tendril and every shape until it was subtle yet unnerving. I manipulated the shadows of the corn stalks, drawing out shapes that could look like fingers or a trick of the mind. It wasn't vivid. It wasn't obvious. But I imagined most unsuspecting viewers would sense that something was wrong with a long enough glance.

I took a break after the sun went down, heading down to my kitchen to make a cup of tea. Decaffeinated, I made sure of it. I heard a *ping* from my phone and checked it to find a single message from Adrian.

'Did you eat anything today?'

I glanced up at the nearby window, pushing the curtain aside. Adrian was out on his porch again, smoking while lying on his back against the bare wood surface. He had his phone in one hand, and I could faintly see the way his head turned toward my window as soon as I answered him.

'Not yet, but soon. Promise.'

He smirked at me from a distance. Even a lawn's width away, I could see that stupid fucking smile and the way he held his cigarette between his teeth while he typed.

'That's my girl.'

Even in text, I could sense the smug tone of voice, and it almost made me regret responding to him in the first place. And yet, I didn't immediately shut the blinds either. This truce was a delicate thing, pinning me between two desires without ever choosing a concrete answer: to let Adrian in, or to lock him out for good? I didn't know what I wanted. By the time I decided, it could very well be too late.

It was the time of night when I paced around my house a lot, walking from one end to the other and looking out every window. Toward the road, I saw nothing but slow-moving traffic and streetlamps that painted the concrete with a rusty yellow glow. Toward Adrian's house, I saw the dim flicker of a television through his bedroom window. But toward the backyard, where my property sat up against a long stretch of cornfield, I saw something new.

One of the stalks was moving independently of the rest, but

only for a moment. I was certain something was out there, peeking from the field and then inching back between the rows of corn once it was found. I put my teacup down, both hands now against the glass. I waited, heart hammering away and breath coming in short pants. Nothing was there now.

There wasn't even a breeze. For the few moments I stood there, the outside world was startlingly quiet; it was as still and as haunting as the painting it had inspired.

"I'm losing my mind," I whispered to myself. This house, this town, this view was driving me insane with every day I stayed here.

It was a diorama of all the things that hurt me growing up. The children who used to bully me for being quiet and strange were now grown, posting beige-colored baby announcements and opening photography studios on every corner. The rest were mechanics and factory workers. My mom still lived on the other side of town, but we never spoke. Last I knew, she still visited my dad in prison every weekend.

I thought back to Adrian again, wondering how on earth we became friends. It was pretty obvious, actually. He was transferred to a bigger school district before we were old enough to get to know each other so that he could get better accommodations. Dyslexia, he said. We were so young and everything was so new, I barely even noticed he was gone.

More than once, he said we would have been best friends back then if we had stayed in the same school. I respectfully disagreed. It was a blessing for both of us that I had missed out on his rebellious, angry teenage years and he had missed out on my mopiest phases. *"I would have stood up for you,"* he said once while lounging around in my living room after helping me move a couch. *"Probably would have gotten expelled for beating someone up, but it would have kept them off your back. Right?"*

But now, I sipped at my tea, eyes still fixed on the cornfield. Some days, it was tempting to just get in my car and drive as far away as I could. It wouldn't be hard to start over somewhere new, would it? My work could go with me anywhere. All I needed was a bed, a kitchen, a place to paint...

And yet, the image of the open road with nothing concrete to hold onto – no goal, no safety net, no structure – was too intimidating to even begin. It would never happen, and I knew this. I couldn't even leave my fucking porch.

When I slept that night, my dreams were restless. My home was filled with noise and motion. An hour before sunrise, I was startled awake by a *bang* from above my head, so sudden and quick that I couldn't tell if it was inside a dream or not.

It was happening again. I stared at the ceiling, completely still, listening to scratching from behind the walls. It moved from one end of the room to the other, random and clumsy like something big trying to fit through a narrow gap. Reaching for my phone, I hesitated to dial 9-1-1. Before I hit that button, I remembered the last time. *Squirrels*, they said. *No sign of forced entry.*

After staring at my bedroom door for a half-hour, I finally mustered up the courage to tip-toe my way to the hall, hearing a tapping sound coming from the other side of the door. When I finally noticed the crooked branches of an oak tree smacking into the window, I felt stupid. Ridiculous. I remembered wanting to call someone about getting that tree trimmed ages ago, but my dumb ass never did it. I was always just too busy.

This time, when I walked into my studio in the morning, I didn't hesitate to look at the painting. I thought that after putting the shadow back into the piece, I would have satisfied that secret need my sleepwalking self longed for. But when I sat down in front of the easel with my morning coffee, putting my hair back with a headband, I froze. Something was different.

It was the smallest change. I almost didn't notice it. The shadow remained exactly where it was the night before, but now two white pinpricks had been placed where a face might be. Slowly, my eyes wandered down to the palette, where a thin white brush sat stained with white paint.

"Fuck," I whispered to myself as I quickly poured a thinning solution to soak the paintbrush for a while. The whole time, my hands were shaking. I didn't do that. I hadn't slept long enough to do that.

"You're done," I said with a disgruntled sigh, picking up the canvas and dragging it over to the closet. I draped it in plastic and laid it on top of a high shelf, somewhere out of reach, where it could sit and wait until I was ready to look at it again.

That day, I started a new project to get my mind off of it. This one was more my usual style: a painting of a long, dark hallway based on the one outside my studio, with half of a face peeking in from the second-story window. Two long, pale hands were curled around the edge to show that the window was open, heightening the dread for observant viewers.

And yet, even as I absorbed myself in the outline of this new piece, my eyes kept wandering to my own window. The sky was getting cloudier as the rain rolled in, long droplets hitting the glass and sliding down slowly. The ambience was perfect for my work, and yet, all I could pay attention to was the way the wind made the rows of corn move in perfect sheets that twisted like the path of a snake.

I shut the blinds, making the room just a little bit darker. It didn't stop the obsession slowly growing in my mind, drawing my eyes back to that spot even when I knew that I would see nothing at all. It didn't stop my racing thoughts or the habitual need to pace back and forth across the studio. But it did make it darker.

My new painting was still in its early phases when I stopped for the night, putting everything back in its place. By the time I put on my pajamas and washed my face, I had a message waiting for me on my phone.

'Wanna smoke?' It was Adrian.

'I don't feel like going out tonight,' I messaged back.

Almost immediately, he responded. *'Then I'll come to you.'*

He made those ten steps from one house to the other quickly, ringing the doorbell before I even had a chance to put my phone on the charger. My pulse quickened as soon as I imagined taking a step outside, even if it was just to stand on the porch in the dark. But if it didn't feel safe inside, what was trading one anxiety for another?

I drew my sweater closer as I cracked open the front door and stepped down onto the cold, rough wood. Even with slippers on, I could feel the chill against my ankles. Adrian was already sitting on the edge of the porch, his feet dangling down about three inches above the wildflower garden I had sprinkled with seeds when I first moved in.

"When's the last time you stepped out?" he asked, watching

the uncomfortably slow pace with which I closed the door. I looked both ways as if crossing the street, glancing down one end of the sidewalk and then the other before finally deciding to take a seat next to him.

"Three, four months ago?" I said, unsure myself. "It didn't go well. I'm assuming reaching out to grab the mail doesn't count either."

"It doesn't," Adrian answered, lighting up a joint between his fingers and taking a quick puff before handing it over to me.

"Will this make me sleepy?" I asked.

"Probably," he smiled, smoke spilling between his teeth. "I told you that you needed more sleep."

I put the joint to my lips and took a small drag, just to acclimate my airways to the heat and the tickle. It was still a little bit wet from Adrian's tongue. "So this was all a part of your master plan," I said, staring out into the dimly-lit street. "You devious bitch."

Adrian laughed at the insult. It was a sharp cackle that could have only been improved if he rubbed his hands together like a fly, perhaps donning a comically villainous eye patch. "Extreme measures for extreme problems," he said. "Gotta put your ass to sleep one way or another so I don't lose my best customer."

"Oh, so that's what this is about," I said, rolling my eyes. "You don't want me to drop dead so you can keep buying my groceries for me. And here I thought you just cared about me a little bit."

"Ew." Adrian screwed up his face and stuck his tongue out. "Care about you? Nasty. Gross. Stop before I throw up–"

"If you're gonna throw up, do it on your own porch," I chuckled and nudged him a little with my shoulder. My body felt heavy and sleepy, and I lay back to stretch out against the cold, hard surface. It was still a little damp from the rain, but I didn't mind it. Most of the rain was currently hitting the roof and rolling off the sides of the overhang above us, making the front yard look as if it had been hidden behind a sheet.

"Adrian?" I broke the silence with a soft, curious tone. "Do you believe in ghosts?"

He didn't even flinch at the question, but I saw the way his smile lines stretched. "Hell yeah, I do," he said. "I've seen a ghost before."

It wasn't the answer I was expecting, but I couldn't resist the lure. "Got a good ghost story for me?"

He grinned as if he had been waiting for someone to ask him that for ages. "As a matter of fact, I do." His voice dropped to a conspiratorial whisper. "When I was a kid, I used to wake up in the middle of the night a lot. I always felt like something was watching me sleep. And then, one night, I saw something." He paused for a smoke, letting the dramatic tension build. "I saw a shape at the foot of my bed. At first, I thought it was a pile of clothes or something, but then it moved. It was rising up slowly, until I saw a pair of eyes staring at me over my feet. Big, wide, round eyes. Like, the details were almost human, but not quite."

"Jesus Christ," I whispered, grimacing. "Sure it wasn't someone playing a prank on you?"

"Mom worked nights," he said.

"Dog?"

"Didn't have a dog."

"Guess it was a ghost then," I shrugged, and Adrian laughed.

"Did it ever come back?"

He was staring off into space now, his eyes half-lidded in sleepy contentment. "No," he finally said. "But I felt it, like someone was watching me when I went up the stairs at night. Sometimes, I'd scare myself thinking it was going to chase me." He laughed. "I still run up the stairs after I turn the light off. My heart starts thumping like crazy." To make his point, he punched a fist against his chest four times in a row. "It's stupid, huh?"

"Not at all," I answered, still lying on my back and looking up at him. "I think it's normal to be scared of being chased. And big dogs. And wide, open spaces."

Adrian decided to lie down next to me, turning his head so that we were facing each other. "And storms?" he asked.

"Are you scared of storms?" I was wearing a shitty smirk that rivaled his.

"Oh yeah," he nodded. "Terrified. You can't possibly expect me to sleep alone on a night like this, can you?"

His words were accented by a crack of lightning and distant thunder, lighting up the sky just long enough to see the glint of his eyes and his teeth. The heavy rain had all but hidden the view of the lamp posts, turning my home into an island.

Adrian handed me the joint again after taking a puff himself, and I took a longer drag this time. I held it in my mouth for a moment before breathing it out slowly, handing it back. But when he took it from me with his lips instead of his fingers, we made the kind of eye contact that froze my body in place. For a split second, my fingers were pressed to his mouth, feeling warm skin and the tickle of coarse, dark stubble.

I hated the way he looked into my eyes the moment we touched, as if casting a spell that kept me rooted in place. Moments later, Adrian pulled the joint away and leaned closer, the smoke on his breath forming a cloud between us as his lips inched closer to mine. The first press of skin against skin was soft, his lips slightly chapped and his cheeks cold. He didn't kiss me for very long. It was like an experiment. But when he went in for a second kiss, getting no resistance from me, I could feel a victorious smile pull at the corners of his lips.

We pulled apart slowly, a lingering sense of numbness on my lips from the pressure. From his point of view, I was sure I looked conflicted: expression blank, mouth slightly open, staring at his individual features one at a time. In reality, I was wondering why it had taken me so long to kiss him in the first place, and whether or not it would ever happen again.

"I was gonna ask if I could stay the night," Adrian said in a soft, low voice, "but you look like you're high as fuck right now."

I cracked a wide smile. The laugh that left my throat caught me off guard and made me hiccup. "I'm a lightweight," I explained. "Besides, I've been having nightmares like crazy lately. I don't want you here for that. Might kick you."

Adrian, still lying on his side and watching me in the darkness, wore a proud smile. "Next time, then," he promised.

He didn't push. I liked that he didn't push.

"When you come over next, I want to paint you," I said after a long, easy silence. "You have a good face for portraits." Adrian, who usually had a smartass comment for everything, looked simply delighted at the idea without any witty retort.

Instead, he just beamed. Genuine. Appreciative. I don't think he was used to compliments.

"I'd like that a lot."

For a while, we watched the rain and the occasional flash of lightning, all while he played with my hair and I fidgeted with a loose thread on his shirt. One thought was stuck on the tip of my tongue, but I couldn't get it out: *I want to leave.* God, I wanted to say it so badly, knowing that Adrian would pack his things that night and go with me to whatever corner of the world I asked for.

But if that request slipped out, I couldn't take it back. And despite the suffocating horror of this prison I had created for myself, I didn't feel ready to go.

Adrian left when we both started yawning, borrowing an umbrella I had stuffed away in the closet. Clumsy and half-asleep, I locked up the house and trudged up the stairs, peeking in at my studio one last time. Everything was right where I left it, perfect and still.

That night, I fell asleep face down on the pillow without even drawing down my blankets. I didn't dream about creatures in my walls or shadows in the corners of my house, stalking me from room to room. I didn't dream about anything.

But just like always, I found myself waking at four o'clock in the morning, hearing a soft tapping somewhere in my bedroom. It wasn't above my head this time. It wasn't in the attic. I opened my eyes slowly, face still pressed against a cool pillow, and turned my head to the side to squint into the corner closest to the window.

For a moment, I couldn't breathe. Something was there. What first could have passed for a shadow cast by the curtain quickly morphed into something more solid, more human, as it moved. Its motions were subtle. It swayed a little, pressing its weight from foot to foot. Low, heavy breathing filled the otherwise silent space until its rhythm matched my own. The thing had no face, but I knew it was watching me. Staring at me. It probably had been for hours.

I opened my mouth to speak, torn between begging the thing to leave or asking why it followed me. Instead, all that came out was a soft whimper. That little sound was enough to get its attention and its curiosity.

The thing standing in the corner inched a little closer, crouched down to get to my level. I watched a hand slide up to the edge of the bed, fingers tangled in the sheets. It tugged just a tiny bit. When I felt the fabric slide against my skin, my hands reached for my bedside lamp in a moment of panicked desperation.

Light filled the room, soft and yellow. My legs moved on their own to push my body against the headboard until my back was flat and my limbs were pulled up tight. The corner was abandoned now. The window was still locked tight, the door was closed, and all I could hear was the settling of the house and my lungs struggling to fill. The shadow, whether it be a ghost or hallucination, was gone.

"You're fucking high," I reminded myself, hands against my forehead. The world was still spinning around me. "You're a lightweight, you dumbass."

I stayed awake in my bed until the sun came up, jumping at every tiny sound. I wanted so badly to fall back asleep, but the memory of that hand sliding toward me across the sheets kept my eyes pried open like metal clamps. And when morning came, my stomach hurt. I walked, stiff and barefoot, down the hallway and to the kitchen. I didn't feel like coffee – the mere thought of its bitter taste just made the pain in my gut feel even worse. Instead, I brought a cup of tea upstairs with me, dunking the teabag as I went.

At first glance, I was relieved to see that the canvas sitting on my easel was the same as I had left it the day before, unfinished but still entirely mine. With a grateful, calming breath, I tied my apron around my waist and set my tea down next to my chair, ready to grab my paint water and refill it. The moment I went to grab it, however, the color of the water gave me pause.

It was red. I didn't remember using red.

In my mind, I was retracing my steps from the day before, trying to recall what I had done from the moment I got up to the moment I went to sleep. Maybe I forgot to clean the cup. No, of course not. I always emptied the water when I started a new piece. Maybe one of my brushes still had a bit of red stuck to its bristles from the painting I had abandoned. But then again, no, I would *never*.

The room was lighter than I expected it to be. Once the cup was placed back where I found it, I took a moment to watch the shadows from the trees dance on the wooden floor. The curtains were open, letting the sun filter in.

With an itch in my brain and an ache in my belly that was worsening by the second, I marched over to the closet and found the abandoned painting still wrapped in plastic, but jostled as if thrown in with a careless hand. I didn't want to look at it. There was no pride in feeling this way, paranoid and anxious about the tiniest of details, but I couldn't help myself from grabbing the canvas and pulling it out just to alleviate my fears.

When the plastic fell away, the painting in my hands looked

disgustingly unfamiliar. My blood curdled when I saw the shadow again – the same one I had tried to cover – now closer than it had been before. No longer was it peering through the stalks of corn. Now, it stood at the edge of the field, two white eyes fixed on the viewer, its feet dangling just an inch above the ground. Bright, thick red paint had been splattered on the corn stalks behind it with an amateur hand.

For the longest time, I stared into those two white dots in the center of the shadow's face, as if expecting it to blink before I looked away. It wasn't well-painted. It didn't match the rest of the image. But somehow, it looked alive.

This time, when I wrapped the painting up in plastic, I took it straight to the garbage can.

My head was still pounding. My stomach had gone from aching to nauseous. Desperate to get away from my studio, I went back downstairs to pace back and forth in my living room, typing away at my phone. I placed an order for Adrian: a home security camera that I could put upstairs to see what happened in the night. All I needed was that evidence, that one piece of definite proof that I had been driving myself insane this whole time. Then, and only then, could I put this shit to bed.

He didn't respond right away, but I didn't expect him to. He had other places to be, other orders to run. That fantasy popped into my head again, the one of the two of us getting in the car and driving somewhere far away where the hauntings of our past could never find us. Deep down, I think we were never meant to stay here. I certainly wasn't.

For the rest of the day, I didn't want to do anything. I didn't want to draw, I didn't want to paint. I locked the studio door from the outside and refused to go back in, feeling my house getting smaller with me inside. Would this continue, I wondered? Would these spaces that used to be safe slowly continue to chip away, one by one, until none of these walls felt like home?

I was sitting on the couch, watching mindless television, when Adrian finally stopped by. He rang the doorbell and waited for me to greet him, standing on the porch in a flannel shirt with a patch on one elbow. He had a single plastic bag in one hand and the other was fidgeting with his phone.

"'Sup," he said, his smile spreading from ear to ear. "Got your camera. Mind if I come in?"

I took the bag when he handed it over, but I didn't budge from the doorway. For a second, I hesitated, almost ready to step aside. Something stopped me. "It's not a good night," I said apologetically. "Sorry, just … I don't think I feel like company right now."

"Gotcha, gotcha," Adrian said with a laugh. "I see how it is – you make out with a guy on the porch and suddenly you're playing hard to get. I've got my eye on you."

When he pointed at my face, wearing a roguish wink, I couldn't muster up the motivation for a smile to humor him. Instead, I shook my head, wincing a little at his joking tone. "It's not about that," I said. "Just a bad night. I promise, you didn't do anything–"

His mood shifted suddenly when he realized I wasn't reciprocating his energy. He leaned against the doorframe, not enough to let himself into the house but enough to keep me from closing the door. "Hey," he said, reaching out to touch my elbow. "What's goin' on, babe? You're freaked out."

Deep down, I didn't want to tell him anything. No matter what I said, I sounded like a crazy person. That was when I reminded myself that Adrian already knew the worst of it: my months of solitude, my fear of leaving the house, the trauma of my childhood that put me here. Letting him in on one more secret wouldn't chase him away.

"Do you remember what you told me, about seeing a ghost at the foot of your bed?" I asked, voice just above a whisper. "I think I've got one here too."

Adrian stared at me, his expression blank and dumb. For a second there, I could tell that he was trying hard not to laugh. But when he figured out I wasn't joking, he gave a singular, awkward nod and shuffled a bit from foot to foot. "That's, uh, pretty fuckin' spooky," he said with a dry, uncomfortable chuckle. "This have anything to do with the camera you asked for?"

I nodded while wrapping my arms tighter around myself, the air feeling colder as a breeze tickled my neck and made the windchimes sing. "Yeah," I whispered. "Things are getting moved around at night. I've been seeing a shadow figure in my room. I just wanna catch it on camera to prove I'm not crazy."

"I getcha," Adrian nodded. "You might catch something wild, right? Listen, the one I got for you hooks up to some kind of app or whatever. You can control it remotely. Move it around, record video, take pictures. S'long as you set that up, I'm sure you can go back and see what's going on." The hand that once touched my elbow slid down to my wrist, subtly cradling our fingers together. "Need help getting it installed?"

I saw the attempt he was making, and I appreciated it. Had I been in a less neurotic mood, I probably would have let him in. "I think I can handle it," I told him. "We'll get dinner soon, okay? I promise."

From the way he leaned in just a little, I could tell Adrian wanted to kiss me. He held back when I didn't meet him halfway, and the look of subtle, biting disappointment on his face made me regret my hesitance immediately. But it was too late to take it back. "I'll hold you to it," he said, "but if you get spooked in the middle of the night, you call me. Got it?"

"I will," I assured him with a nod, knowing full well that I probably wouldn't. "I'm gonna go to bed early, I think. Have a good night."

"Yeah, you too." Adrian didn't break eye contact until the door was closed. I could still see him as he walked past the window, shuffling back to his own house while talking under his breath. I could only imagine what he was saying: hating me, regretting his pursuit of me, voicing his quiet frustrations. But no. He wasn't like that.

The guilt and embarrassment aside, I got to work putting the camera up immediately. The box was a little banged up, I noticed, but all the pieces were right where they were supposed to be. Sitting on my bed, setting up an app to catch a ghost in my house, made me feel silly. And yet, I didn't know any other way.

That night, I couldn't sleep. I paced around the hallways again and again, checking my phone to see myself on the night vision camera as a small, tangible comfort. What wasn't comforting was the view of my bright, blank eyes and washed-out skin, hair looking frizzier and wilder than ever. Walking around in an oversized t-shirt with bare feet, I looked like a feral thing in black and white. Every image of my face looked as if I had been caught in the wild. It was a view of myself that I never imagined would be so chilling.

That night seemed to go on forever. I paced around the studio, making sure nothing was amiss. I inspected every lock, every window, every *inch* of my home, finding only stillness and an uneasy quiet. I spent an hour staring at my current painting, trying to force some kind of inspiration to work – I was too exhausted to pick up a brush, but too wired to sleep.

Nothing was here. No one was here.

I finally fell into bed near two o'clock in the morning, lying face-down with a pillow over my head. All I could hear was my own breathing, my pulse in my ears. The comfort of being in my own little handmade isolation chamber finally helped me drift off to sleep, but I didn't stay that way for long.

Ever since I was young, I had always been a light sleeper. I became accustomed to waking up at every little sound: shouting from my parents' room, doors slamming, the sound of crying, a weight on the edge of my bed. Sometimes, my dreams were so vivid that I could still hear all of it. I could still feel it. This time, it was that weight that woke me up.

My eyes were still closed when I began to drift back into my body. At first, the weight of someone sitting on the edge of my bed could have been an illusion. And then, a slight shift made it a reality. It was just a tiny motion, the quiet creak of old springs. The pillow was still positioned over my head, but I could feel that eerie, suffocating sensation of someone's body heat mingling with mine. The oxygen was being sucked out of the room.

The hair on my arms and legs began to tingle, goosebumps forming in an otherwise warm room. I wanted to pull a blanket over my exposed legs, but I worried what would happen if I did. Would the figure sitting on my bed realize I was awake? Would my hand go for the edge of the comforter and touch something else instead, like a cold, dead hand or a gaping mouth full of teeth? That fear paralyzed me, forced me to continue pretending I was still asleep, breathing in a heavy rhythmic pattern.

And yet, I had this feeling in my gut that the stranger already knew. No matter how still I remained, no matter how slowly I breathed, I could feel the weight of the figure looming over me, inching closer as if to inspect every detail.

They moved so slowly. What was more than likely less than a minute felt like the most agonizing hour of my life. First, a light pair of fingertips brushed one of my ankles, gliding up the back of my calf as if testing me. The touch was warm. Alive. I did my very best to remain still and silent until I felt a little nudge against the pillow. One of my eyes cracked open, noticing a hint of moonlight from the window, eclipsed by the head of the intruder. The corner of my pillow was slowly pulled up, a shadow peering beneath it and blocking the light. I couldn't see their eyes, but I was almost positive they saw mine.

When a small, sharp gasp left my throat, the shadow suddenly darted away, slipping beneath the edge of the bed. I heard it shuffle through the darkness, fast and quiet, leaving only the creak of floorboards behind. And this time, the door slammed as they departed.

It took me a few moments to catch my breath, my whole body

shivering with more than panic; it was a deep, overwhelming sense of disgust that made my toes curl and my hair stand on end. I spent a while just sitting on my bed with the lights on, listening to the natural creaks and groans of the house. It was an hour before dawn, and the sunlight couldn't come quick enough. With my phone held tightly in my hand, I eventually left my bedroom while dialing 9-1-1. The operator picked up just as I was taking careful, quiet steps down the staircase.

"My name is Willow Bohmann. Um, 605 South Bolson Street. I-I'm sorry, I know I've called before, but I really think someone was in my house." Even as I tried to keep my voice level, the panic was coming through with each breathless word. "I...I don't think they took anything. Nothing is broken. Just someone watching me sleep. They..."

I paused, and the operator quietly asked if I was still on the line. The phone felt heavier in my hand as I stared at the front door, eyes scanning the locks, then the windows and their tightly secured latches. Finally, I whispered: "I think they're still in here."

The house suddenly felt bigger than ever. There were so many shadows, so many corners, so many places where someone could be hiding. The attic. The basement. I tried to remember the last time I had checked those narrow basement windows; could someone fit through those? I thought about the roof. If someone climbed the maple tree and crawled up to the chimney, then maybe–

I sat on the porch while I waited for the police to show up. The whole time, I was thinking about how tragic this was: the one place that used to feel safe now felt like untamed wilderness, no different from the open spaces that filled my heart with terror. My pulse slowed while I sat outside, legs crossed tightly at the edge of the steps. The lights were off at Adrian's house. He was probably sound asleep, I thought.

Before long, police lights lined the street and my neighbors craned their necks to watch as officers in black inspected every inch of my home with flashlights. I didn't like it. I didn't like them digging around, looking at everything that was mine and mine alone, stomping around each sacred inch of my private space. They checked the security cameras. The footage had been wiped. I didn't delete those videos.

It didn't take long for Adrian to leave his house wearing pajama pants, no shirt, and nothing on his feet. He saw me sitting on the porch and rushed over, cutting through the yard and stepping around the rose bushes. "What happened?" he asked, his face pale. "You okay?"

When Adrian crawled up onto the porch, I scooted a little to make room for him. "Yeah, I'm okay," I said with a tremble in my voice that I couldn't hide. "Someone was in my bedroom, watching me sleep. I-I don't know if it was real or not, but..."

"Jesus fuck," he breathed out. From the way his chest deflated, I could tell his heart was racing with each word. He seemed genuinely scared. "He didn't, like, touch you or anything, did he?"

"No," I answered immediately. "I mean, yes, but barely a tickle. But he didn't hurt me."

Adrian voiced another sigh of relief, slow and shaky. "Good," he said, his hand reaching for mine in a tight squeeze. His fingers were warm, but the rest of him must have been freezing. We sat there for a long time, bathed in red and blue blinking lights until the police finally gave me the answer I expected: *we didn't find anything.*

"It doesn't look like anybody forced their way in," one of the officers said to me. "Did you give anyone an extra key?"

"No," I said, shaking my head. My toes were starting to go numb. "No, I didn't."

"Make any extras to stash around the yard, maybe a spare set? Could someone have stolen one or made a copy?"

I shook my head again, more stern this time. "Definitely not," I said, a little too defensive. "I've only got the one. I-I mean, sure, I lose track of my keys every now and again like everyone else but–" I interrupted myself with a shrug. "N-no one else has one."

They suggested I stay with a friend. They didn't know my situation or the monumental effort it took for me to simply step onto my porch, let alone leave the property line. Adrian offered that I stay with him, as I knew he would, but he didn't seem shocked when I refused.

"Let me stay with you then," he said, standing half-in and half-out of my doorway after the police had left. He put an arm around my shoulders, bringing me in just close enough to brush coarse stubble against my forehead. "You shouldn't be alone, not after that."

Something about the way his fingers dug into my shoulder made me flinch. I pulled away carefully, my arms clamped tight to my sides as an unpleasant itch passed from the base of my spine up to my neck.

"Not this time, okay?" When I spoke, my voice was weaker than I intended. " I'm sorry, I just wanna be alone. For now. Is that okay?"

Adrian's eyes flashed with something between disappointment and annoyance, the second rejection hitting him a little harder than the first. He cleared his throat, and I could tell that moment of self-collection was his attempt at stopping himself from saying something he might regret.

"Yeah, babe, that's okay," he finally said, his hand sliding away from me. "Listen, I'm right next door if you change your mind, okay? And I'll bring you some breakfast in the morning. How's that?"

"You really don't have to–"

"I insist," he interrupted me, already backing up and onto the porch. "Morning. I'll be back to check in."

And this time, I didn't argue. I had already rejected him enough lately. Before he could get too far away, I pulled him in for a tight hug, my face buried snugly just below his left shoulder. He returned it, of course. Even after pushing him away again and again, he never refused me. Maybe we were both the problem.

I locked the door, checking it over and over and over. And every time I walked by, I checked it again. That oak tree was still tapping its longest branches against the upstairs window, still catching me off guard with its shadow.

Once I was alone – truly, silently alone – I checked the security camera upstairs. The view of my studio and the empty hallway was chilling, but a reminder that nothing was waiting for me up there. I stood at the bottom of the stairs, eyes fixed on the way the steps disappeared into a deep, oppressive darkness. Even the window at the end of the hall offered no light, only the distant rumble of a rare train passing through town. I didn't think they ran this late at night.

Every step that I took toward my bedroom was slow and careful. I wasn't alone. No matter how much the police insisted, I knew that something was here with me. Maybe it wasn't human, maybe it wasn't even physical, but it was real and it was here.

I stopped at my studio, staring eye-to-eye with the painting I had been working on. The image of an open window, something crawling through with long, sharp fingers, was hitting me a little too close to home now. I shut and locked the door to keep away the temptation of throwing that painting in the garbage right next to the last one.

Whatever was stalking me – *haunting* me – was only brave enough to come out while I was asleep. With that in mind, I stayed awake as long as I could, keeping my eyes open until the early morning light began creeping through the cracks around the curtains. It was only then, when the sky was orange and yellow and the stars were gone, that I allowed myself to drift into a fitful, brief sleep.

I awoke feeling more tired than I had been before. My stomach was sick, my skin was crawling, and even the foggiest dreams were full of anxieties and violations. The memory of those dreams started to fade the second I opened my eyes, patting around blindly for my phone. It was eleven o'clock.

I had a message waiting for me, and I knew who it would be before I even opened it. Adrian had already been to my doorstep, from the looks of it.

'Why did you throw that painting away?' he texted, roughly an hour before I woke. *'I think it's great. Don't give up on it, okay? I left it by the door for you.'*

"Fucking fantastic…" I groaned as I turned over in bed, stuffing my face into a pillow. It took me another twenty minutes to get out of bed, staggering to the bathroom to brush my teeth and splash cool water in my face.

Still in my pajamas and yawning loudly, arms stretched over my head, I marched down the stairs until I was standing in the dining room, my feet against cold hardwood. For a moment, the memories of the night before faded into the daily mundane: making coffee, doing a few dishes, opening the curtains to let the light in.

I heard another ping on my phone. It was Adrian again.

'You up yet?'

I typed out an answer quickly on the smudged touchscreen.

'Just woke up. Head is killing me.'

I was about to text one more time, telling him not to come over until after I had my shower for the day. But I paused, my eyes drawn to the front door – or rather, the canvas tilted against the wall beside it, still covered in plastic and duct tape. A box of donuts sat on the dining room table just a few feet away.

Another ping. Another message.

'Have a good breakfast, pretty lady. See you soon.'

The Mist Over Superior

I never really knew when to give up. It had been a problem ever since I was young, when Owen and I would challenge each other the way siblings always do. He still reminded me of the day we played hide-and-seek in the woods near the old family farmhouse. For hours, I searched for him, climbing trees and digging through piles of dry leaves, getting thorns stuck in my palms. It wasn't until well after nightfall that our mother came looking for me, telling me that Owen had been in the house all evening, currently watching TV in the living room. I suppose he thought I'd give up eventually.

He was thirty-four when he went missing. He told us he was going up north for a fishing trip, visiting this spot he liked near an old lighthouse on a jagged rock. Owen didn't like speedboats or big, gaudy pontoons. He liked to take his fishing kayak and sit out there in silence, letting the waves dictate where he went. *Superior is a mean old bitch*, he would say whenever he got back. *She can change her mood in an instant, so you've got to know her well.* I went with him once and only once, and he teased me for the way I gripped the sides of the boat with a white-knuckle hold.

When our mother called me on a Monday morning, I knew something was wrong. She usually only called me if someone died or if I had missed a birthday. Owen was always her favorite, after all. He was bolder and more extroverted, he had more friends, he brought home girls that mom and dad liked. He got a good job working at a machine shop by recommendation of a family friend, and had been there long enough to become a supervisor. By comparison, I was a wanderer. I moved from one job to another, I hadn't bought a house, I didn't have a partner. I sank into the background, no different than the furniture and antiques that collected dust in our old family home.

"Owen hasn't called," she told me that day. *"He always lets me know when he gets back from a trip. Did he call you?"*

He didn't. Deep down, I think she knew that he didn't. She was just desperate enough to ask.

There was a search party and a full investigation that lasted a month. Our parents went on the news, begging for him to call home just to tell them that he was okay. We offered a reward for anyone who had seen him. About a week later, we were offering a reward for any-one who had found his body. And by the time one month had rolled around, we were just begging for any evidence that he had been there at all.

I didn't understand how every single hint of Owen could be gone: no body, no boat, no fishing rod, no anything. When I talked to folks who lived up north, they told me it was just what Superior did. She didn't give up her dead. When she had you, she kept you – something to do with the temperature in the water being too cold to let bodies rise to the surface. If my brother was truly dead, he was now a preserved, frigid statue covered in corpse wax somewhere on the bottom of the lake, sitting there like a rock.

But a part of me didn't want to believe that. I couldn't fathom that after years of sailing those same waters, exploring every bay, and learning the moods and patterns of Superior, my brother would get taken out by a tricky current or a shock of cold water. He was better than that. He was luckier than that.

In the end, I was the last one looking for him. When Mom and Dad didn't call anymore, I still looked. When his friends bought an extra beer at the bar in his memory, I was still collecting maps of the bay and circling islands where his kayak might have drifted off to. Maybe it was because we were twins. There was some secret tether between us, making sure we never strayed too far from one another. I could still feel it, tight and tingling like an electric wire that wouldn't snap. A shared umbilical cord that fed us both.

When I left, I didn't tell anyone. I took a few days off work and headed off on a long drive, sticking close to the shore for the scenic route. My aging Buick, which rumbled when I accelerated too fast and squeaked whenever I closed the passenger door, took me north of Keweenaw Bay and alongside the Bete Gris Wetlands Preserve.

Arriving at the coast didn't feel the way I thought it would. Whenever I imagined the place where my brother died, I pictured a desolate and silent patch of wilderness, miles from where anyone could possibly hear him. Instead, I found autumn colors and trickling waterfalls, SUV's parked in every overlook with mountain bikes strapped to the back. I found families having picnics and strangers stopping for drinks at the gas station, talking about the next destination on their 'color tour'. It was far too cold for swimming. Fishermen were still flocking, though, picking up bait while talking about the ice fishing season ahead.

When I stopped for gas and coffee, I silently listened in on these conversations, all while staring face-to-face with the same kind of chewing tobacco my brother used to buy. He only got it when he was fishing. It wasn't as much a habit as it was a tradition, I guess. I bought a can, a tiny, dark voice in the back of my head telling me to stuff it in his coat pocket the day we finally pull his body up from the bottom of the lake.

"Is that it?" the woman at the counter asked. She had weathered skin but the thickest, curliest blonde hair I had ever seen.

"Just this, and thirty dollars on pump three," I told her. "By the way, I was hoping to rent a boat somewhere around the point east of here. Know any places?"

The lady took my money and sifted through it, counting out my change. "You'll go to Ted's Lakeside Rentals if you want a pontoon, but you'll pay for it."

"I'd rather have something small just for a day," I told her. "I'm not throwing a party or anything."

The lady thought about it for a moment, then slid the tobacco across the counter toward me. I pocketed it along with the receipt. "I think the campground a few miles east has 'em available if you spend the night. Keweenaw's got rentals too. Just make sure to get something sturdy."

"That's perfect," I said, breathing out a sigh. "Thank you."

"Sure thing, hon." She had already begun ringing up the old fisherman behind me by the time I took a step away, just long enough for me to pick up the scent of tobacco and lake water.

The mid-afternoon sun blinded me the moment I stepped outside, minding the sudden curb. And while I filled up my car, one hand in my pocket to keep my fingers warm, I noticed the man at the pump next to me. He stood completely still, his neck tilted back, staring up at the underside of the canopy. I glanced up and saw only spiderwebs and grime. If it were summer, there'd probably be droves of mayflies.

But when I put the nozzle back and grabbed my receipt, that man still hadn't moved. He didn't even blink. Instead, he was whistling a tune, still gazing up at the canopy while his body swayed ever-so-slightly from side to side like a branch being nudged by the wind. When I looked closer, my eyes taking him in from head to toe, I realized his clothes and hair were damp. Had he just been on the lake? I moved behind the pillar just a step while putting the gas cap back in place, but I couldn't escape the eerie feeling that he would move closer if I took my eyes off him.

Once I got back in my car and started the engine, I spared him one last glance before pulling away. He was holding the nozzle in one hand and letting it drip onto the ground, forming a dark, glistening puddle next to his shoes. He watched me leave, his head turning to follow me, all while his lips formed words I couldn't hear. The whites of his eyes were brighter than they should have been.

My heart rate only slowed as soon as I knew I was out of sight. Something about him was wrong. His eyes were a bit too wide, pupils too small, mouth open too slack. He hadn't even blinked when water dripped from his hair down to his face.

"Guess they've got tweakers here too," I said to myself while a shiver went down my spine. Thankfully, the trip around the point had stunning views, bright autumnal colors, sparkling waters, and the occasional family of deer. It wasn't long before I wasn't thinking about that man at the gas station anymore. Instead, I was thinking about how happy my brother must have been to spend his final days here on a warm summer morning. It was probably beautiful.

The beaches were quieter now than they were back then. When I finally arrived at the state park where my brother had last been seen, I stepped out and immediately felt the cold wind coming in from the water. The waves were loud and frothy, leaving the sand and rocks bearing a dark, wet stain. I pulled my jacket in a little tighter, thinking back on Superior's frigid temperatures. This time of year, the water on the surface was still a bit warmer than the air around it. Underneath, however, in the deepest parts of that freshwater sea, centuries of wrecked ships and passengers slept in a frozen grave that could never be disturbed.

Winter was just beginning. Soon, the shoreline would freeze and any chance of finding Owen would be gone.

I found a dry, jagged rock and climbed onto it, cursing quietly when my boot slipped and nearly dunked into the water. Finally, when I was sitting atop the rock and watching the waves lick against the surface just below me, I took a moment to simply enjoy the view. When I paid no attention to the trees and the beach, it looked almost endless. Almost.

In the distance, perched on a small island that was otherwise completely deserted, a little wooden lighthouse stood by itself against a gray horizon. Even from far away, I could tell that it was old and falling apart. There was an isolated, forgotten beauty about the way it seemed to fade into the mist that surrounded it. I imagined on a foggy day, it would disappear completely.

On a hot summer's day, though? That little island was probably a charming landmark against a perfect blue sky. The greenery on the rocks probably shone gold against the harsh sunlight. A few fluffy white clouds would dot the sky, moving slowly and catching the orange and red light of morning. Owen would have loved to take his boat around the island just to grab a few photos. Maybe he did, I thought.

I took a few pictures myself, after crawling down slowly from my rock like a mermaid with a hangover. Some of the photos were just for aesthetics, enjoying a rare view of autumn leaves hanging over rolling waves. Other photos were a record of where the waves crashed against the shore, where debris was washed up when twigs and branches got caught in the current, and how far the beach stretched. And still, my eyes kept being drawn to that lighthouse.

The sunset over Lake Superior was something else entirely. From one side of the point, I couldn't see anything except the glimmer of orange and red light through the trees. But when I walked along the beach that stretched south, that western sun finally peeked over the water and left the waves bathed in gold glitter. I took a few more photos. Grief was a strange and foolish thing, I realized, as my fingertips automatically found my brother's number with the temptation to send the pictures to him. He would have loved them.

I sat in that spot until the sun went down completely. No one bothered me, no one asked me to leave. The beach was far too cold for swimmers or picnics. And as the sky grew dark and the stars appeared above me, unburdened by streetlamps or city lights, I felt a kind of peace that didn't exist anywhere else.

I wasn't alone, though.

Before long, I heard a low whistle coming from the water. It was a song – something kind of formless and casual. It was followed by the gentle lapping of waves against a rocking boat. He came into view slowly. A man, sitting alone in a rowboat that was far too small for these unpredictable waters, gently began to drift by under the soft light of a half-moon.

For a while, I just watched him. I couldn't make out his features or his face, only a black silhouette with a hat against the dark water. He rowed so slowly, at first I wondered if it was moving him at all or if the waves were just pushing him along. And yet, he never seemed to get any closer to the shore.

The whistle was soft at times, then shrill. When it would echo over the rocks, a tingle went from the base of my spine all the way to the back of my neck.

Eventually, he stopped rowing. He stopped whistling too. He sat there in the water, the waves gently rippling by without moving him closer or further from where I sat. A voyeuristic sense of wrong-ness came over me. Maybe I shouldn't be here. Maybe he should be alone. Deciding that I would give this man the beach to himself and find a new spot to perch, I shifted on the rocks and stuck my feet in the sand.

But when I stood up at long last, keeping my eyes on the man in the water, I watched his head turn slowly in my direction. Against the blackness of his silhouette, I saw his eyes: bright, white, glowing like two little beacons against a dark sky. Perfectly round. The suddenness of it caught me so off guard that I dropped my phone, fumbling with it before it had a chance to fall into the water.

"Shit!" I hissed, pocketing it quickly. My eyes had been off the man in the boat for less than three seconds, but in that time, he disappeared. Somewhere beyond the rocks and the trees, I could still hear that shrill whistle. It got further and further away as the waves took him to another section of lonely beach.

Once the man was gone, I felt a truly profound sense of isolation. It was just me, the water, and the shadow of that tiny lighthouse in the distance. I could only tell where it was because of the way it blocked out the stars and the glittering water behind it. Sometimes, moonlight would catch one of the waves that crashed against the island, far more violent and active than the shore.

The moon continued its trip from one side of the sky to the other. I stood there until the man's whistling had faded completely, but I could still hear it in my memory – a familiar tune, one that I simply couldn't place. It lived in my brain, tucked behind years of disorganized memories. There was a good chance I'd never know where it came from.

That night, I stayed in a shitty motel with a rabbit ear TV and cigarette stains on the ceiling. It reminded me so much of the house we grew up in. Our grandfather would smoke even though he used an oxygen tank, and our mother would tell him to stop before he blew up the whole damn house. Owen would put on a dramatic show and pretend to take cover under a couch cushion. I was a nervous child, afraid of everything, but that would always make me laugh.

While I was lying in that motel bed, flipping channels and listening to the muffled conversations through the walls, I thought about Owen a lot. Maybe he would be proud of me for being here. He always did say that I didn't get out enough. *You're so pale we don't even look alike anymore,* he would tell me every time he got back from a summer trip with tanktop-shaped tan lines.

I still had a voicemail from him saved on my phone, sent a few days before we realized something was wrong. Right after he went missing, I was afraid to listen to it, as if I had to somehow preserve the last time I heard his voice. That night, however, I finally let it play.

"Hey, dork, I'm gonna come up this weekend to visit mom and dad. You gonna be there for dinner Sunday? Listen, maybe afterwards, we can go see a movie or something. I feel like we never get any time, just the two of us. Well, anyway, I gotta get back to work, but we'll talk again soon. Miss you, buddy."

I had deleted every other voicemail except for that one. In the motel, I listened to it several times in a row, memorizing the tone of his voice all over again, trying to imagine the view he must have seen as he called me from the edge of the lake. He was probably holding the phone in one hand and a tackle box in the other. With each passing month, he sounded more and more like a stranger to me, and I feared the day I heard his voice and didn't recognize it the way I used to.

I left the room to grab a pop from the vending machine outside. It must have been raining after I settled in, because the sidewalk connecting all of the rooms was slightly damp. Droplets were rolling off the fire escape and gathering in puddles, the gutters still draining slowly.

I cursed under my breath when the machine didn't want to take my dollars. Happy that no one else was around to watch me struggle, I flattened the bills against the faded Pepsi machine several times in a row before the wrinkles were finally smoothed out. It took a few more tries before I finally heard the lucky clatter of a can falling to the bottom. When I bent down to pick it up, reaching deep inside with my head tilted, I noticed someone standing in the parking lot.

She was facing away from me, wearing a puffy coat and lingering near the curb as if waiting for someone to pick her up. She swayed a little bit. At first, I thought it was just because she was older and perhaps a little unsteady on her feet. But moments later, I watched her begin to turn, her head leaning back so far that I could see the lump in the center of her throat.

Immediately, I was reminded of the man at the gas station. The looseness of her posture, the way her limbs were hanging limply at her sides, the gentle sway of her body that told me she could fall over at any moment; and yet, she was held up by an invisible tether, one that kept her wide open eyes on the sky. Wiry gray hair cascaded over her shoulders like a witch from a storybook.

"Ma'am, are you okay?" I called out, standing up straight with a pop can in my hand. "Do you need me to call a ride for you?"

When I got a step closer, I noticed that the woman was sopping wet. Her coat, her hair, even her shoes were drenched and oozing water that collected at her feet in a wide, ever-growing puddle. And when her head tilted back even more, her spine bending at an unnatural angle, I saw her wide-open mouth, collecting rain drops that fell from the motel roof. I noticed how her eyes were a little too big, too bright. Her arms were just a bit too long. Her hands, which once looked wrinkled from a distance, were water-logged and blue with black grime beneath her nails.

I started to step back, my gaze locked on her. Any hope of going unnoticed was lost the moment her pale eyes snapped in my direction, fixing me with a cold and unrelenting stare. Shoving my wallet back in my pocket with clumsy hands, I turned and began to walk back to the door, swiping my key card. It blinked red at first, my fingers too shaky to get a good read. But when I tried a second time, I became aware of the slow, quiet slaps of wet feet against the concrete behind me.

I felt a chill when I turned my head, almost wishing I didn't. The old woman had moved and was now standing behind a tree. At first, I could only see her wispy white hair and the edge of her coat, but she began to lean ever-so-slowly until one bright, shining eye found me. Her pupils were so small I could barely see them. The whites of her eyes seemed to glow.

The card reader clicked and I pushed the door open without hesitation, pushing it shut as quickly as I could. The woman didn't pursue me. She didn't even move. But as I pressed my back against the door, clutching a can in one hand so tightly that the aluminum began to bend, I could hear the muffled sound of the old woman whistling a tune.

I went straight to my room, heart pounding. There was a logical explanation for all of this, I told myself. Drugs. Dementia. Sure, it was unusual that it had happened twice in the same day, but I didn't know this place. Maybe this town was full of freaks and it was normal to everyone else.

As much as I hated to be a bother, I did the only thing that made sense at the time: I called the front desk, telling them there was a confused woman standing outside the motel in the rain.

"She's old, probably ... seventy?" I said, standing next to the outdated, cream-colored motel phone. "She was confused and soaking wet, probably freezing. She looked sick. I dunno, I figured if she's got dementia and is having an aggressive episode, there's no telling where she'll end up next."

I felt stupid, being afraid of an old woman. I shouldn't have run away from her. A responsible, more level-headed person would have stayed and tried to subdue her long enough to call someone on the spot, but every hour I spent by this goddamn lake seemed to make me feel less and less rational.

They didn't find the old lady. I didn't think that they would. But once I was done watching flashlights drift over the parking lot, I shut the curtains and crawled into a stiff bed with a thin, scratchy blanket. I stared at the ceiling for hours. Now and again, I swore I heard the light tapping of fingertips on the window, but I didn't want to turn and look. It was probably raindrops.

But the rain didn't explain the soft, muffled whistle that I heard as I began to drift off to sleep. A whistle from wet, cold lips.

Superior looked different in the afternoon sun. The waves were calmer, the light was yellow and glittering against cool water. The rain from the night before had dried up, leaving only shallow puddles that collected against the deepest grooves and dips of the pavement.

There were handprints on my window. I only noticed them

when I left. I think the man at the front desk noticed the way my fingers shook as I fumbled for my keys at the door, but he didn't ask about it. It was a relief to leave.

I ended up stopping at that little rental place the gas station clerk had mentioned the day before. When I got there, surrounded by fishermen and hikers who all seemed much more knowledgeable than I, one of the employees must have agreed that I was out of place. While I wandered aimlessly, staring empty-eyed like a time traveler at the wrong stop, a young man with an orange hunting beanie waved me down.

"Need anything specific?"

"I'm looking to get a kayak, maybe for today and tomorrow," I said, fidgeting with my wallet out of habit. "And, uh, do you know if they do any tours around that lighthouse on the rock?"

The employee walked me back to the desk, making a thoughtful sound along the way. "Gashkawan Rock?" he asked. "I don't think so. They stopped doing tours there years ago, probably because it's way too old. Someone fell through the floor, I think." He didn't seem fazed one bit. "Did you want a one-person kayak or a two-person?"

"Oh, uh, just one," I answered, holding up an index finger. It was habit by now; my voice was notoriously soft, hard to hear. "And I just bring this back at the end of the weekend?"

"That's right," the young man grabbed a heavy set of keys from off the wall while he spoke. "It'll be seventy-five for today and tomorrow. If you don't bring it back by closing time tomorrow night, you pay full price for the kayak on top of that. Two hundred and fifty in total."

"That sounds fair," I breathed out the words, fidgeting with the snap on my wallet.

I paid and followed the kid out to the back, helping him strap the kayak to the top of my car. That bright sun was starting to disappear as thick clouds rolled in, not quite the color of rain. We got the bungee cords nice and tight. I wondered if the rust on the sides would chip and somehow send it all flying, but once I got back on the road, it felt sturdier than I had expected.

Thinking about sailing without my brother for the first time left me with mixed feelings. I wasn't sure if he would see it as an honor or a betrayal, me carrying on a tradition with him in mind. But when I sat on that rock at the edge of the water, listening to his voicemail one more time before getting the kayak in the water, I liked to imagine that he would just want to be found. No matter what.

It took me way too long to get the damn thing off the top of my car, and even longer to pull it out to the water by myself and get it where I needed it to be. I was overly cautious with every part of the process. No dings, no dents. It was a pain in the ass to maneuver around the rocks and the tree roots that had started to inch into the water's edge. But once it was there, pushing it into the deeper water was easy.

Tours around the rocks had ended for the day. There were no more people fishing by the shore or exploring around the hiking trail. A long dock with a few benches stretched out into the deep water, but it was far enough away that I could barely make out the tiny silhouettes of walkers on an evening date. The sun went down early this time of year. It left me alone with the cold waves and distant thunder from a passing storm cloud to the west.

I shivered when my boots and the bottom half of my pants

were soaked with lake water. The first cold rush was bad enough, and the chilly wind made it so much worse. But once I began to paddle my way further from the coast, I saw the appeal of the freezing air and the tumultuous waters.

Being out here alone felt endless. The setting sun was casting the most beautiful colors across the waves, and its glow reflected off the windows of the distant lighthouse in such a way that it almost looked alive again. I could picture Owen out here so easily. He'd probably be rocking the kayak back and forth, pretending to capsize just to tease me – just to make me scared. I was starting to miss the behavior I once hated.

Further and further into the water I went, paddling quickly at first and then taking it slow. The waves were calm that night. I saw a few very distant sailboats and the lights from town, but they twinkled like faraway stars.

Once I was nowhere near the shore, the loneliness was unlike anything I had ever known. Out there after nightfall, miles from unnatural light, it was just me and the deep, dark waters. That little lighthouse was closer now, no longer illuminated by the setting sun. Instead, it wore a soft blue glow given to it by the moon. A light mist was rolling in.

And somewhere out there, hidden in the layer of fog that was rising over the water, I heard a whistle again. This time, it was far away and closer to shore. The same place as last time. And just like the night before, the song sounded so familiar to me. It was driving me mad.

I turned in my seat and saw that little rowboat again. It was drifting from the shore and toward the deeper waters, heading straight for me. But it was slow. It was so slow that it never got any closer. From far away, I could see those pale, white eyes against a black silhouette, and it made my heart race with terror to imagine that the man sitting in that boat saw me better than I saw him.

"Fuck…" I whispered under my breath, paddling further away. Maybe if I got around the lighthouse, he wouldn't see me. Maybe he wasn't pursuing me at all.

My arms were starting to hurt and the rock was still so far away. When those waves got a little rougher, I felt how far away from shore I really was now. Looking down, the water was black as ink and the mist from every wave was freezing cold. I imagined that if I tipped over right now, I'd have to swim a long ways before I found a place to put my feet. The bottom of the lake was so far down.

Shoulders burned. Lungs ached. I turned around once to see if that man was still following me, and I noticed that the paddles of his rowboat weren't even moving. And yet, he was just as close to me as he was before, staring in my direction and whistling a tune.

When my back was turned and I began to row again, faster than before, I heard a new voice.

"I feel like we never get any time, just the two of us."

The hair on the back of my neck stood on end and I looked in each direction. "Owen?" I asked, reaching for my phone with one hand while laying the paddles on my lap with the other. My fingers were frozen and I was shaking.

My phone wasn't turning on. The battery had died at some point once I got onto the water.

Before I could even stuff my phone back into my pocket, I heard Owen's voice again. It was a perfect imitation of what I had heard so many times before on that voicemail, crackling in my ear when I listened to it over and over again in the middle of the night. Only now, it was coming from behind me.

"Well, anyway, I gotta get back to work, but we'll talk again soon." This time, I realized where it was coming from. The man in the boat had stopped whistling, and now he was speaking, his face obscured so I couldn't even see his mouth move in the dark. *"Miss you, buddy. I feel like we never get any time, just the two of us. Miss you, buddy."*

When he began repeating words and phrases, always in the exact same tone of voice, my stomach felt sick. Those glowing white eyes had never looked more malicious, more menacing. I started rowing faster, breathing heavily with my collar up over my mouth to keep the chill out of my lungs. I was coughing. Every time I turned around, the man was never closer or further away. It was almost like he and I were held together by an invisible string – an umbilical cord that couldn't be cut.

The lighthouse was looming over me now. I paddled fast, trying to fight against the rocking waves as Superior pushed against me. Gichigami herself was trying to drive me away. But with the rocks in my reach, I pushed on, listening to that voice over my shoulder as it echoed over the rolling water. *"Miss you, buddy. We'll talk again soon. Miss you, buddy."*

It's not him. It can't be him. If it was Owen, he would have said so. He would have called out to me, he would have said my name, he would have told me to wait for him, he would have–

"We'll talk soon, buddy. Miss you again. Miss you."

It was mixing up the words now, making new sentences, but

it still sounded alien to its lips. I don't think it knew what the words meant. It? Yes, it. There was no way this thing was anything but 'it'.

Finally, the water was growing shallow near the rocks. The waves were still violent, pushing me further from the shore, but I managed to find a way around where I could hook onto the jagged edge of the island. The rocks scraped against the side of the kayak in a way that made my ears hurt. With a grunt, I pushed myself out of the boat and grabbed it by the nose, pulling it up with me as I climbed the slippery, wet rocks. Once or twice, my boots slid off and dunked back into the icy water. My teeth chattered, but I was determined to pull it the whole way. If I lost it now, I'd never get it back.

After endless struggle and freezing, sore hands, the kayak was sitting nestled between two rocks so that it couldn't float away. I gave it a few kicks to make sure it wouldn't budge. It was trapped tightly. The moment I could pull my eyes away from it, I climbed a little higher to peek over the island's summit, looking for that man in the rowboat. He was still out there. He was circling the island, still a football field's distance away from me, still watching with predatory curiosity.

His voice was muffled by the waves, but I could make out those chopped and senseless words.

"Come up. Mom and dad. We never get any time, just the two of us. We'll talk again soon. Again, just the two of us. Miss you, buddy."

I started to hike up to the lighthouse, that voice following me the whole way. It faded as soon as the walls of the building stood in the way, but I knew it would only be a matter of time before he circled the other side of the island.

The cashier was right about the lighthouse. It was old as hell, the paint long chipped and the wood rotting. Windows were broken, the stairs leading up to the front door had fallen through, and the tower seemed to tip when I looked at it from a certain angle. Absent-mindedly, I grabbed for my phone. "Shit," I whispered, remembering that it was dead. No flashlight. In my hasty efforts to get out here and look for Owen, I hadn't been very prepared.

Even without a light, I found that the lighthouse door was open. The cloudy sky had drifted west and now the moonlight was shining just enough so that I could see the room around me in a cool, blue hue. I had to give my eyes a moment. There was a small wooden table in the center of the room with three chairs around it. The fourth was knocked over and lying on its side with a broken leg. Everything was shorter than I was used to. I suppose, back when this place was built, furniture was smaller and rooms were more narrow.

There were plates on the table and a loaf of bread still sitting in the center, long-molded and crumbled until now it resembled a stone. I ran my fingers through a layer of dust, thick and cold. It looked like ash on my skin. It was thickest on the table itself, the tin cups, and plates that still had the suggestion of petrified food scattered on top. So thick that I could see very clear, very obvious handprints from someone who came before me.

Someone else had been here. Of course they had. Just because they didn't do tours anymore didn't mean no one had broken in to explore the place. I turned around in a circle, looking at the cracked windows and the scuffed floors. As my eyes continued to adjust to the subtle moonlight, I noticed things I didn't see before.

There were handprints on the windows and dark stains on

the door. There were areas where the dust had been wiped away as if something large had been dragged across the room from one end to the other. The staircase leading up to the light had a massive hole in the center, splintered wood in all directions. The cashier did say that someone had fallen through.

A little gasp left my throat when I heard that whistle again. The man in the boat had circled the island and was now closer to the lighthouse, his silhouette visible through one of the windows that viewed the open water. He looked so eerie out there, a black speck against an otherwise endless horizon with no land in sight. The white glow of his eyes found me in an instant, and I ducked down beneath the window to hide from his gaze.

He'd be waiting for me as soon as I left. I knew that. But for now, he seemed content to circle and watch, knowing that I had to come out eventually.

While sitting on the floor, my ass frozen solid on top of dust and rotting wood, I saw something underneath the dining table that caught my eye. The moonlight bounced off the edge of something metal and shining – something *new*. I did a little army crawl over to it and picked it up with both hands, turning it over and over. It was a keychain. It was ordinary to look at, with a set of car keys, house keys, and a gas station savings card. I knew this keychain. I had seen it before. On the short lanyard loop, there was a Detroit Red Wings enamel pin. Years ago, Owen had bought it when we went downstate to catch a hockey game with mom and dad.

"My God…" I whispered under my breath, turning the keychain over between my fingers. "You were here. Owen?" I raised my voice. "Owen!"

I felt stupid. He wasn't here anymore, there was no way. That feeling in my gut came back again, tight and itching like claws reaching into my body and pulling me in. He was close by and I knew it. We could never be too far apart. As I sat under the table and looked at the keychain, remembering the way he'd jingle it in the air before leaving the house, my eyes were misty from tears and dust. Fuck, I missed him so much. I wanted my other half back, and no one – *no one* – had even tried to find him the way I did.

Why didn't they care? Why didn't they miss him too? Maybe it was because we were in the same womb, growing side-by-side from nothingness. And no matter how much I despised his boldness, his loud voice, his repetitive jokes, or his exhausting energy, I still wanted us to die the way we were born: together, always.

I shoved the keys in my pocket, wiping my eyes with the sleeve of my jacket. My arm had been dragged through dust, and it stung when I realized my mistake. "Shit!" I cussed as I wiped my face again, looking for any clean, dry bit of fabric. The tears left on my skin felt cold enough to freeze.

My nose was running. My eyes burned. When I stood up, I bonked my head on the table and felt like a complete and utter wreck. That man outside was still whistling, but he stopped to speak again when he saw the top of my head through the window. *"Miss you, buddy. Just the two of us. Miss you."*

I couldn't leave, not yet. I needed to know if Owen was still in here, waiting for me somewhere, even if he was just a pile of bones and dusty clothes. With renewed energy, I made my way to the narrow staircase, taken aback by how steep the steps were. Every step I took was shaky, the wood creaking and snapping beneath my feet. But I was too far up to turn back now.

He was up there. I knew he was.

The stairs made a tight spiral, ending in a crooked archway that was covered in hanging cobwebs. I pushed them aside to protect my eyes. Up there, high above the island rocks, I was face-to-face with the abandoned light that once used to reach for miles over the water. The view was ... everything. I saw the land in the distance, the lights of the towns, the tops of trees, the natural landmarks and waterfalls. To the other side, I saw nothing but miles and miles of deep water.

The floor beneath me was covered in dust, dirt, and the faded hint of boot prints. They were frantic and random. The glass around the light was stained and covered in grime, but hands had been pressed against it at some point. In a moment of sentimental desperation, I stepped over scattered ropes and bags of sand to put my own palms up to the surface, comparing the size of those hands to my own. Until that moment, I hadn't even noticed the way my lungs could barely find breath.

"Owen?" I called out his name again, knowing I'd get no answer.

But this time, I did.

"Miss you, buddy." The voice was closer now. It wasn't coming from outside or muffled through walls and waves. It was coming from behind me. Slowly, I turned my head to look down that narrow stairway, my eyes searching the spot where the spiral turned a sharp corner. A black, oppressive shadow bled onto the floor and the wall from a spot where the moonlight couldn't touch.

I heard a creak on the steps.

"Are you there?" I asked, bottom lip trembling. Tears were running down my face again. My knees wobbled and my stomach felt sick with anxiety. "Owen?"

"Are you there?" the voice spoke back to me, its tone just as tearful as my own. It didn't sound like Owen anymore. *"Just the two of us. I miss you, buddy."* I heard it take another step and the shadow moved, longer and closer to the wall. *"Are you there?"* it repeated.

When it took a step closer, I took a step back, jumping when I smacked right into the light's cold, hard surface. The shadow on the stairs had stopped moving again. Instead, I could hear a low, hoarse breathing. It was rhythmic and wet, reminding me too much of how the waves sounded when they crashed on the rocks.

The stairs creaked again. That shadow was getting closer. This time, I finally saw a silhouette peek around the corner, two white eyes shining against an otherwise pitch black form. I let out a shout of terror and the thing darted away, but not before the steps beneath its feet splintered and collapsed.

"No," I whimpered as the fear inside my heart took new shape. "No, no, no!"

Without thinking of the figure at all, I rushed toward the edge of the stairs and looked down, watching wooden planks and rusted nails clatter the whole way down. It left a gaping, endless pit that was impossible to jump. The room I stood in, high above the ground with only the dead light to keep me company, was now an island in the air.

"Oh, God, no," I whispered as I crawled closer to the edge. The wood beneath my knees and my hands shivered. One wrong move and my prison would shrink even more. "Owen? Owen!" I called my brother's name desperately. "Owen, I'm up here! Please!"

The voice answered me, now further away. *"Just the two of us. Please."*

I stood up and paced the room with frantic energy, looking for a way out. There was rope scattered everywhere. With a rush of victorious confidence, I grabbed a piece and held it up, giving it an experimental tug. With just a little force, it frayed and snapped in my hands, rotten through to the center. The short, fragile bits left behind would never get me down. Heart plummeting, I let the pieces fall from between my fingers.

Rushing toward the window, I pounded my hands against it to see if it would crack. Maybe I could scream. Maybe I could wave my hands and someone would see me throught he mist.

That man in the boat was no longer circling. I saw him, now sitting in a kayak exactly like the one I had brought with me, paddling away slowly as he made his way toward the deeper waters. He glanced back to look at me, unblinking eyes like two stars against a black sky before he finally turned and faded into the mist that had surrounded the island.

My back slid down the thick glass window. For the first time, I felt truly alone in every way. Reaching into my pocket, I held my brother's keychain, realizing how cold it was against my fingers. I could see my breath in the air now. My knuckles were aching and my skin was red and chapped.

They didn't do tours around the lighthouse anymore.

The Shoe Tree

I still go home from time to time, out to the old farmhouse my grandfather built. It sits between a long cornfield and a patch of woods that comes right up to the back of the yard. There's an ancient stump out there where I liked to sit and smoke, and a mint garden that comes back every year no matter what you do. No one lives there now.

I didn't have the heart to buy it, knowing that the view from the back window would always remind me of the last time I ever saw my best friend. He was a weird kid, the kind who would steal candy from the gas station just to let it melt in his pockets. The kind who would jump in the ditch to catch frogs and get sick every single time.

Shane and I spent a lot of fall weekends camping in the woods behind my house, following a path we made ourselves. Our favorite spot was this thick, overgrown area between a noisy creek and the skeleton of what used to be a one-room schoolhouse that was barely standing. It was perfect: just far enough in to block out the sound of traffic, but not so far that we couldn't get home. Shane tossed me a note in class one day, little doodles all over it and 'Nate' in big, blocky cartoon letters. *'Camping this weekend?'* the note read. He was grinning at me from across the room, chewing on his pencil and punching holes in his eraser while his schoolwork remained untouched.

It was 1997. September, I think. And between the news of Princess Diana's death and the first screening of *Titanic*, something happened in a little Michigan town that the rest of the world would never hear about.

After school, Shane and I rode our bikes home together almost every day. He lived in the trailer park right outside town, and my family's farmhouse was a little further down the same dirt road. He always asked to come over and hang out at my place. He said it was because I was the only one with a PlayStation *and* a Nintendo 64, but I had met his dad enough times to know that wasn't the reason.

Keith Webber was a piece of shit and everyone knew it. The man's man that he was, he lived on a diet of cheeseburgers and beer, but not that low-calorie stuff. He said that shit would push your balls back up into your body. When Shane didn't make the junior football team, his dad punished him by breaking his arm — *allegedly*. Mr. Webber said he wiped out on his bike, but we all knew better. His bike wouldn't make a bruise shaped like two sets of fingerprints.

We usually tried to get home early so that Keith didn't throw a monumental fit. That September day, however, Shane and I took the long way 'round. I followed him, our bike tires cutting through piles of dead leaves and puddles from an early morning thunderstorm. The smell of worms and mud was still heavy.

"I wanna show you somethin'," he said, looking over his shoulder. He was weaving back and forth across the road, splashing water in either direction.

I followed his pattern, making a game out of it and picturing an imaginary trail. "It's not another one of your dad's weird magazine collections, is it?" I grimaced. Shane laughed and shook his head, turning a corner onto a long dirt road flanked by soybean fields.

"Nah, it's way weirder than that," he said with glee. He picked up the pace, making the sounds of squealing tires as he hopped his bike over rocks and valleys, pretending to be a BMX cyclist. He nearly ate shit a few times and had to correct his balance, but he was nothing if not persistent. With dark clouds rolling in and no cars in sight, we rode out of town and to a patch of woods where the narrow dirty path began to curve like a snake. There were no traffic signs out here. No lights.

Shane stopped, drifting into a pile of leaves and almost falling on his ass. When he stood up and brushed himself off, he pointed to the biggest tree on the roadside. "It's a shoe tree!" he said. "There's a few out here, but this one's the big guy."

The sight he gestured to was a massive, gnarled, dying tree with no leaves and no fresh growth. The moss growing on its trunk was its only green. In lieu of life, there were hundreds of shoes with their laces tied together, tossed in the air to be caught on its branches. Most of the shoes were older than we were, either bleached from the sun or falling apart from rot and weather.

It had no reason to creep me out so much, but it did. The way the tree leaned to one side, burdened by the weight of its purpose, made me a little sad. If the tree had been a living person, I would have imagined it to be stooped over in pain.

"I don't get it," I said as I nudged my kickstand into place.

"You don't need to *get* it, stupid," Shane chuckled. "It's just, uh … like an urban legend. A tradition." He walked over to the tree, hopping over a fallen branch. I watched as he climbed, getting dirt on his knees and his hands. The tree itself seemed to groan and creak in protest, dry limbs wobbling in a way that made me cringe. When Shane got to the first big branch, he swung his legs over it and sat a few feet above the ground.

"A kid from the trailer park told me about it," he continued. "He said a serial killer used to live out here. He would hide in the woods, and whenever kids would walk down this dirt road alone – wham! He'd smash 'em to death with a hammer and throw their bloody shoes up into the tree. Now his ghost haunts the woods, and people leave shoes as an offering."

I climbed after him, pulling myself up on the opposite branch until we were both kicking our legs. "An offering for what?"

"Just, like … so he doesn't come back and kill you too or whatever," Shane said with a shrug. We weren't very high up, but the view already looked different. It wasn't bad. The wind had picked up, sending dry leaves rolling across the dirt, and those dark clouds were moving a little faster now. The cornfield across the road was waving at us. I could see the path of the wind as it moved east, pushing the dry husks in a gentle pattern. Another thunderstorm was coming.

"What was the killer's name?" I asked.

Shane shrugged dramatically and made a face. "I dunno."

"Wouldn't there be, like, articles about it? In the news?"

"Fuck, I don't know, it's just a story."

"So it's bullshit," I chuckled. "That's really stupid. Next you're gonna tell me you're afraid of a shoe ghost?"

"I'm not afraid of him, jackass," Shane argued. "It's a story the older boys made up so they can bully stupid little kids by makin' em walk home barefoot. Never worked on me, though." And just to prove me wrong, I watched him shimmy further down the branch and snatch a pair of blue running shoes that were about his size. A couple of twigs snapped and clattered down the trunk as he worked to untangle the strings, frayed and stained from the weather. Despite the stress his weight put on the branches, Shane didn't even flinch at the thought of falling.

"See?" He held the shoes up. "I ain't afraid of no dead kid-killer. But if *you're* scared, you can leave your shoes behind to appease him—"

"No way," I scoffed. "This is my only good pair. Mom will kick my ass."

We both jumped down from the tree, Shane going straight for a pile of leaves while I swung from my hands first for a cleaner, less hazardous landing. While I was wiping the dusty residue off my hands, Shane was already getting back on his bike, the shoes now dangling off one handle.

The ride home was quick with the wind at our backs. We beat the storm clouds by a few minutes and pulled into the long, bumpy driveway to the trailer park.

His place was on the left, standing out from the rest thanks to the sheer amount of trash on his lawn and the rusted car parts his dad would leave in the yellow, flattened grass. Shane always said his dad was good with cars and wanted to fix up the busted Mustang he kept under a tarp, but I had never seen the man work on anything. As far as I knew, all he did was drink beer, watch TV, and scream at his son for breathing.

"Dad's not home yet," Shane said, and I could hear the undertone of relief. "You wanna hang out for a bit? I've got an airsoft gun, we can shoot some cans. Oh! We can play *Duck Hunt!*"

"That game is from, like, years ago," I said, rubbing the back of my neck with a dismissive laugh. "But I already told my mom I wouldn't be home late tonight. Sorry, man."

"No, no, that's cool," Shane shrugged. His eyes wandered to the ground and he transferred his weight from one foot to another. He never truly wanted to say goodbye, but today was different. The wind was blowing colder.

"Maybe next time," I offered. "Soon, okay? Tomorrow?"

Shane wore a brighter smile, but it didn't quite reach his eyes. "Yeah, let's do tomorrow." He bumped his fist against mine. And when our half-baked idea of a handshake eventually turned to just slapping at one another without rhyme or reason, I finally decided it was time to go home.

"I'll see you at school," I told him, kicking a pile of leaves toward him. He kicked it right back.

"Yeah, see you," he waved. He looped the stolen shoes over his shoulder and stepped into the trailer, the door screeching while I glimpsed peeling wallpaper and cigarette butts ground into the scratchy blue carpet. The distinct sour odor of neglected trash hit my nose from several feet away.

I got home just in time. The storm followed me, swirling dark clouds and distant thunder heralding my arrival while I parked my bike in the garage. Dad wasn't home yet. Mom was on the phone, speaking up over the drone of a soap opera while she folded dry towels in the living room. The floor was freshly vacuumed, judging by the lines still left on the off-white carpet. Back then, my mom had these terrible, floral-printed throw pillows and a wall covered in decorative plates of all different designs and sizes that she got from flea markets. I hated them with a passion.

My mom noticed me before I had a chance to slip by. "Oh, hold on, Cheryl, Nathan just got home. Nathan!" When she shouted my name, I flinched.

"Hey, mom," I said, half-hidden behind the wall. It wasn't good enough — she could spot a grass stain from a mile away.

"Nathanial!" she huffed, looking me up and down with the phone receiver silenced against her chest. She spoke in a hoarse whisper that was both quiet and biting. "I just washed those pants!"

"I'm sorry, I was playing with—"

"It's fine," she said sharply, "just...change and put them in the hamper. I'll take care of it." She groaned and put the phone back to her ear. "I'm still here, Cheryl. Yes, everything's fine. Nathan's been outside playing."

When I went upstairs, changing out of my dirty clothes and into a pair of sweatpants instead, I hid myself away for an hour by telling my mom I was doing homework. That was true, for a while. When I couldn't focus on my math booklet, I played *Super Mario 64* and kept the volume low enough that my mom wouldn't be able to hear it. Even back then, the flat geometric textures and eerie open spaces made the game feel scarier than it should have been. Something about the repeating shapes, the open blue sky, and the loneliness of it all made my heart beat faster.

That night at dinner, I wasn't hungry. I pushed my food around while Mom and Dad talked about their day, and it wasn't until I refused the mashed potatoes that my mother asked if something was wrong.

"Are you sick?" she asked, reaching over to touch my forehead. I flinched away when she messed with my hair, shaking my head so that the center part fell back into place.

"No, I feel fine," I lied. "Just got a lot on my mind, is all."

My dad let out a knowing huff, probably imagining all the same things he worried about when he was a middle school boy. My mother, on the other hand, put down her fork and knife to give me her full attention. Even when she was being caring, her expression carried a calculated type of chill that made me feel like the subject of an interrogation.

"Did something happen after school? You were late getting home."

"I was playing with Shane," I told her. The reaction was immediate. She rolled her eyes and shook her head, giving my dad a disappointed glare that insulted Shane in ten different ways without saying anything. But she didn't stop there.

"I wish you wouldn't spend time with that boy," she said, stabbing at her pork chop. "He *shoplifts* from the gas station, for God's sake. Maureen's daughter works there, she's seen him do it." She crinkled her nose in distaste. "You need to start making some better friends, Nathanial."

My dad tried to interject. "It's not the kid's fault that his dad didn't teach him any manners. Keith was the same way when I was in school with him." He gave me the kind of subtle smile that told me he was trying to help. "Maybe Nathan is a good influence."

My mother was glaring daggers at my dad now, and I realized that maybe I had made a huge mistake by saying anything at all.

And yet, I couldn't help but spit out what had been on my mind.

"Mom?" I asked, my voice timid as I tested the waters. "What if ... what if we let Shane stay here with us for a while? His dad is really mean to him."

My mother was about to take another bite of her dinner when she clicked her tongue and crossed both arms in front of her chest, leaning forward against the table. She was annoyed before, but this was a new level. "We *cannot* let him stay here," she said, her tone final. "It's not our business, honey. I know you just want to help, but there are some things you should not stick your nose in, okay? Besides, where is he going to stay? The dog house? By all means, if you want to give him your room, go right ahead–"

"Julie, you're not being fair–" my father tried to interrupt, but my mom's mind was already made up. One glance from her was enough to shush us both. Looking back now, I understand why my mom was so set in her ways. She was trying to protect me. If I had known the extent of Shane's fucked up family life, I probably would have taken him to the police station and done the responsible thing instead.

But I was a kid. These were adults. Why didn't anyone *do* anything?

"I'm going to bed early," I finally said. My stomach was still empty, but I chose hunger over this fruitless argument. When I pushed my plate away, no one resisted. No one told me to stay.

That cold, violent wind was still out there, shaking the power lines and making the tree branches quake. While I bundled underneath my blankets, the twigs tapped at my windows, startling me awake every time I fell asleep. Quick flashes of lightning lit up the sky and made the shadows of our old, gnarled oak tree look like claws outside my bedroom. I had never been afraid of it before. Well, maybe it scared me when I was a baby, but I couldn't remember a time when I turned away from the windows and closed my eyes as tightly as I did that night.

The nightmares I had were terrible: hands reaching through the window to grab me, a rotten, ghoulish face, ghosts circling my bed while I slept. Sometimes, I imagined the rain tapping on the window wasn't rain at all. They were long, decaying fingers, knocking to get my attention while an inhuman face smiled at me from the other side. I pictured that same dead and water-logged thing breathing against the glass while staring at me with wide, empty eyes. Hungry. Eager.

In my imagination, looking at it would break the spell that protected me. If we locked eyes, it would come inside and get me. That was my logic. So long as I stayed awake, kept my eyes closed tightly, and kept my back to the window, I would be safe.

Daylight couldn't come fast enough.

I walked to school the next morning and got there late. My mom thought I was sick, my dad thought I was up all night playing video games, and I could tell from the moment I walked into class that Shane hadn't slept either. He was sitting with his head down on the desk, unwashed dark hair covering his face while he hid himself behind a book. He sat in the back row, hoping the teacher wouldn't notice he was napping. She did. Now that I look back on it, she probably knew more about his situation than I did. She just let him sleep, shaking him gently when it was time for him to leave. I was standing in the doorway when she touched his arm and called him 'sweetie'. Even that gentle, light nudge was enough to make him flinch.

During lunch, he didn't talk to me. I tried to wave him down, giving him a big smile, but his eyes never left the floor. I watched him throw his food in the trash can and grab his bag, walking straight out of the building. For a second there, I was tempted to follow him. I decided against it. He disappeared, going off to find some quiet place to be alone, probably to sit on the Elementary playground and sip at a beer he stole from his dad's fridge. My mother's words echoed in my head then, reminding me that there was nothing I could do. I was too young to question her then, too young to realize that my friend simply didn't know how to ask for help.

For the first time, Shane rode home without me. By the time I unlocked my bike chain and started to ride down the sidewalk, he was already gone, his figure blending with a misty afternoon drizzle.

And for the second night in a row, I barely slept. A terrible smell was stuck in my nose, and at first I thought a mouse had died under my bed. I couldn't find the source. It only got stronger, thicker, more oppressive as the night went on, prompting me to open the window and let the cool air drift inside. From the second story, I could see a view of the woods and the cornfield. The wind was moving through the crops in waves again. In my sleep-deprived state, it almost looked like the trees were walking toward me, sentient and purposeful.

Everyone has that moment as a child when they realize how big and scary the world is. For some people, it's seeing a brand new landscape on a long road trip. For others, maybe it's learning about the passage of time and the age of the earth itself, knowing just how many people and animals came before us. But that moment at the window was mine. Picturing the forest itself out to get me, slow and patient and old, made me realize just how powerless I really was.

That was the first time I ever felt afraid to go into the woods.

When morning came and I began packing for my camping trip with Shane, I dreaded going out there. I almost didn't go at all, and a little part of me hoped he would call soon and tell me he wasn't feeling well. But when he showed up, gear strapped to his back and a tired, grim look on his face, I knew I couldn't let him go all alone.

He was pale and a little sweaty, wearing a tight beanie with greasy hair sticking out of the sides. His flannel shirt was hanging off of him and wrinkled as if it hadn't been washed in a few weeks. The faint scent of stale laundry and beer stuck to him.

"Dude, are you sure you should be out here?" I asked, following behind Shane as we walked through the field. "You look really sick. Maybe you need—"

"I want to go," he interrupted me. "I...I want to go." His voice was stern, his jaw tight. "And I'd rather not go home right now. Dad is in one of his moods."

"What's his problem now?" I asked, stepping over a heavy fallen log. I was expecting one of the usual answers — Keith was drunk, he had a bad day at work, Shane left his bike out, or something else stupid and insignificant. But instead, Shane went quiet for a long time before speaking in a hushed, shaky voice.

"I've been having these nightmares," he said. "I woke up screaming. I've never done that before, and dad got pissed." He went quiet while we reached the treeline, finding that little path where the greenery was flattened down. I whistled a tune to fill the silence, but the way the sound echoed off the trees made my skin crawl.

Shane was silent and stone-faced while we looked for a spot to set up our tent. While I took my backpack off and started to clear some leaves away with my foot, Shane was dropping loud metal pipes and stakes to the ground, kicking them around to get them exactly where he wanted them. Finally, he spoke up again. "He's gonna kill me one of these days. It doesn't matter, though."

I wanted to tell him that it did matter. I wanted to tell him that I had always noticed the bruises, the scrapes, the sick days from school, the way he deflated when he had to go home. And I wanted him to know that I tried to save him. I tried. Those words, as empathetic as they were, wouldn't help him right now.

We worked together to put the tent up, communicating through glances and muscle memory alone. And when it was done, we built a little spot to put a fire together, surrounding the pit of dirt with stones to keep it all in one place. It took a while to find branches that weren't damp from the storms, but a cigarette lighter and some dead twigs did the trick – right on time, too. It was starting to get dark.

The fire was small, but it was warm. The orange, flickering light licked the edges of Shane's face, showing hollow cheeks and deep sockets that were aged beyond his years. He was jumpy that night. I could see the whites of his eyes darting from side to side as he shivered at every sound and whisper of wind. My friend was always a bit twitchy. It was one of the main reasons he got picked on in school so much. Tonight, though, he was on high alert as if the walls were closing in.

"So, you haven't been sleeping either, huh?" I asked, poking the fire with a long stick. "I've been having bad dreams too."

"What about?" Shane started pestering the fire with his own sharp, skinny twig.

"Just...creepy noises at night, I guess," I explained with a shrug, trying to act casual about it. I didn't want him to think I was a coward. "Monsters outside the window, someone watching me sleep, that sort of thing. Super weird."

On any other day, he probably would have laughed and called me a pussy for getting scared of a silly bad dream. Monsters, slashers, and ghosts were the kinds of things that scared little babies. But this time, I watched the gears turn in Shane's head as he stared into the fire, his breath shallow. He was shaking, but it wasn't even that cold.

"The monsters came into my room," he finally said. His voice was soft and deadly serious. "I had a dream that something crawled through my window, and when I woke up, it was actually there, standing over me, reaching out for me. It's hard to describe what it was. It was like ... I don't know. Something dark with lots of arms and eyeballs all over. That's when I started screaming."

He took the beanie off his head for the first time that day, revealing a big, swollen bruise on his forehead with a scab that went vertically above his eyebrow. The skin around it was red and inflamed from infection.

"Jesus," I whispered. "Did your dad do that?"

"I woke him up," Shane told me with a shrug, as if it was the most normal thing. "He told me if it happens again, he'll make me sleep outside. I suppose if I'm gonna be sleepin' outside, I might as well do it out here, camping with your dumb ass." He finally gave me a crooked, toothy smile, but everything about it was fake and forced.

I didn't know what to say, so I didn't say anything. I simply stared into the dwindling fire, thinking about how bad things must have been at home for Shane if he would rather risk the creepy forest than sleep in his own bed. The ghost of an idea started coming to me then. I was his safety, and that responsibility was more than a kid my age was ready to grasp.

In the silence that passed, I was rehearsing words in my head to say to him. But before I had a chance to ask if he ever considered going to the police to show them the wound, he came up with his own idea first.

"Maybe we could stay here," Shane broke the silence. "Live out here in the woods forever."

I let out a bark of laughter that startled even me. "What, like, go feral?"

"Not feral, stupid," Shane gave me a nudge. "Feral kids are, like, born in the woods and shit. I'm saying we could fend for our-selves. Like, um … that book we read. *Lord of the Flies* or whatever. Those kids lived alone without any parents."

"Yeah, and they also ate each other."

Shane blinked at me in the firelight. "Did they really?" he asked.

"I dunno," I gave him a shrug. "I didn't finish it."

And for just a little while, the air between us was lighter. We laughed, we teased, we roasted weenies over the fire, and joked about which one was bigger or more crooked than the other. We talked about how we'd build a huge treehouse and live in the woods forever. Shane would build a gutter on the roof to collect rainwater. I would learn how to hunt. And while I listened to his ideas, all I could think about was how smart this kid could be if someone actually gave him a chance. He could really be something one day.

We knew these ideas would never actually come to life, but for a moment, it was a fun dream. It was an escape.

After an hour by the fire, Shane yawned and stretched his arms over his head with a sharp *crack* of his shoulders. I could only imagine how exhausted he was. "If you start screamin' in your sleep, I might have to kick you out of the tent," I told him. And Shane, always taking things in stride, grinned at that.

"Yeah, well, if you fart in your sleep, I'm throwing you in the creek."

I rolled out my sleeping bag and Shane put down a couple blankets, side by side, pointing in opposite directions. The mesh roof was just thin enough that we could see the stars and the gnarled branches overhead, as well as the buzzing insects that fought to get in and drink our blood in the night. When I found a spot to recline and crossed my arms behind my head, I could just barely see one corner of the moon. Before long, it would be hidden behind the tree branches, too. When I looked over, Shane was lying on his back, and I saw the holes in his dirty old socks peeking from beneath the blanket. He wasn't snoring yet – that's how I knew he was only pretending to be asleep.

"Hey, Nathan?" he finally said, his eyes still closed.

"Yeah, buddy?"

"I'll see you in the morning, okay?" The way he said it sounded hopeful yet desperate, as if he himself wasn't sure if it was the truth. I think he wanted me to reassure him that the sun would come up and he would be okay.

"Yeah, I'll see you in the morning. G'night."

Shane fell asleep first, but something kept me awake. I felt restless and cold, feverishchills going up my spine and stopping at the back of my neck. Whenever I would start to doze off, the memory of those dreams would come back to me. The tree branches above us would remind me of the ones that tapped against my window. The sound of buzzing insects would make me think of that rotten smell. Every animal rustling in the bushes or the treetops sounded like someone – or something – circling our campsite, all while my brain concocted horrible visions of what it could possibly be. Every mental picture was worse than the one before it.

At long last, when the moon had dipped beyond the trees and the clouds, I began to drift off for real. My eyes weren't closed for very long. It was still pitch black in the tent when I was nudged awake by a cold pair of hands, gasping to find Shane just an inch away. His eyes were impossibly wide and all the blood had drained from his face, leaving him ghostly white.

"What the fuck?" I murmured, still half-asleep.

"We have to go," Shane whispered, lips wet with spit. "Get up.

We have to go *now*."

Before I even sat up fully, Shane's head was whipping around in terror as a twig snapped outside our tent. That sound, paired with the wind that made our sanctuary sway, was enough to wake me. I quickly began to shove my shoes on, growing nervous as I watched Shane do the same. His hands were shaking so violently that he could barely keep his hold. At the time, I couldn't tell if I was genuinely scared of whatever was outside our tent or if Shane's anxiety was contagious.

"What was it?" I asked, pulling my jacket on. "A bear?" Shane was lacing his second shoe and grabbing one of the flashlights from his bag.

"I... I saw–" Shane gasped for air, trying to stay quiet. "There's something out there. I-I'll tell you later. We just gotta go."

He unzipped the tent with clumsy, shaking hands and practically threw himself out into the woods, hissing as his knees hit the scattered stones and twigs. The air was cold and the wind was cutting, whistling through dry autumn leaves. There was no moon anymore. As I looked up into the shadows of gnarled tree branches, the starless night sky was like an open void – a door spread wide to *nothing*.

"Come on, move!" Shane was gasping for breath as he shoved my shoulder, urging me to leave everything behind and run. And as my feet began to move, I heard him smacking the flashlight against his hand behind me. It didn't come on. "Fuck!" he yelled, and I heard the tears. "Come on! Fuck, come on!"

The way he screamed, hysterical and half-gagging, almost tempted me to stop running and go back. He sounded unwell. He was freaking out over nothing. But when his flashlight finally came to life and he pointed it into the trees, I heard an unearthly hiss and saw the branches move – no, not the branches. There was something in there. It was tall and thin, the texture of its skin blending in with the nature around it, and it was gone before my eyes could even adjust.

Shane saw it too. More importantly, I think it saw him. He began to yell and weave from one side of the path to the other as if avoiding an obstacle, but it all moved too fast for me to see. We passed by a stack of abandoned cinderblocks next to the schoolhouse. Shane jumped over them, but I fumbled just long enough to catch a loose shoelace on the bottom of my foot and stumbled forward. Despite his panic, Shane paused to pull me back upright.

"We're going the wrong way!" he said, gasping for breath. Those few seconds we spent trying to find the path again gave our pursuer just enough time.

When I turned to look at Shane's terrified face, I watched his flashlight fly out of his hand and into the bushes, tangled up in thorns. In this new level of darkness, Shane's body veered sharply to one side. At first, I couldn't tell if he did it on purpose or not, until I heard the crack of his shoulder against a tree trunk.

There are so many things from that night I'll never be able to forget, but the way he cried is at the top of the list. The shriek in his voice reminded me of a baby, and for a few seconds, he was just a little boy screaming for his mom again. I found him crumpled next to a fallen tree, my eyes finally starting to adjust in near-pitch darkness. But before I even saw him, I could smell him. He was so scared he had wet himself, that ammonia scent blending with fresh blood so strong that I could taste metal in my mouth.

"Shit! Oh shit, are you okay?!" As I shouted at him, my voice sounded muffled by the pounding in my ears. Blood rushed to my head as I grabbed Shane's arm, trying to pull him up to his feet. I felt like I was going to pass out. A light sliver of moonlight appeared between wispy, dark clouds, and I could see the way his other arm dangled, broken near the shoulder. When he moved, he cried harder.

Something had thrown him into the tree. The wound was evidence enough, but more telling than that was the look of dread and terror on his tear-soaked face. I knew that whatever I had seen was nowhere near as terrifying as the view Shane must have had.

"Shane, get the fuck up!" I yelled again, pulling him harder. He stumbled after me, crying so hard he couldn't even open his eyes.

"M-my arm's broken–" he was gasping for air.

"I know, I know it is," I said, pushing him forward. "My mom will take you to the hospital, but we gotta go!"

"It hurts so bad–"

"I know!"

Shane took a few steps, all while something began to circle us. I couldn't even tell what size it was, its body blending with the forest as if it were molding itself to the environment's many shapes. Before long, it wasn't running on the ground anymore, but had scurried up a nearby tree to jump from limb to limb like an animal. It shook the branches as it went, breaking some of them and sending them falling around us.

I held Shane's hand as I dragged him behind me. He didn't run so much as he stumbled, sobbing and babbling half-choked sentences like *"don't leave me"* or *"it hurts so bad"*. There was nothing I could do to comfort him and he knew this. But he begged for comfort still.

"We're almost there." I gave him an empty promise, having no context of how far we were from the path. It all started to look the same. "Come on, just a little further–"

"I don't wanna die!"

"You won't die!" My voice cracked. "You're gonna be fine, we're so close!"

We weren't close. Even running in a straight line, I started to see the same fallen tree again and again, blood still staining the bark where Shane had been thrown. We almost tripped over the cinderblocks. And a few steps further, I spotted the collapsing blue dome that was our abandoned tent. Running away from it didn't matter. We were called back, over and over, never able to get too far.

At that point, Shane was starting to get delirious. His skin, olive-toned and tan from time in the sun, had paled everywhere except for the bruise-colored circles around his eyes. His clumsy steps were turning into a strange, patternless gait that reminded me of a zombie from a horror movie. My skin crawled more when I looked at his arm, hanging limp and loose from one low shoulder with his palm pointed in an impossible direction. It didn't even look like an arm anymore. It barely looked like it was attached to him.

While I tried to run further away from the tent, he was swerving toward it, his heavy breathing getting further away as he shambled through the overgrowth. "Where are you going?!" I asked in a bitter whisper, but he couldn't hear me.

I had no choice but to follow him. I wasn't going to leave him behind to stumble around the pitch black woods on my own. Shane's wobbly legs got him to the edge of the tent, where I watched him hunch over and begin to vomit on the ground next to the doused firepit. He was still crying at the same time, legs shaking as he tried not to fall over into the mess he had just made. I ran toward him and grabbed his shoulders, keeping him upright, holding back his hair. Giving him dignity.

And still, something was out there. I could hear it circling the campsite. It was just *toying* with us now – whoever it was, whatever it was didn't want to pounce just yet. I think it was just watching to see what we would do next.

Getting back in the tent was a bad idea, but Shane attempted one step and began to crumble. He was passing out. When he collapsed onto his knees, holding himself up on one shaky arm, I helped him crawl back into the tent. He immediately fell onto his back, wide eyes staring up at the mesh ceiling. My fingers were trembling something awful as I zipped up the door, giving us a thin, frail layer of protection from the thing that stalked between the birch and oak. It knew we were here. It would find us. It would get us. But for just a minute, we were alone in a place where we could rest.

"Shh, shh, stop crying," I hissed at Shane, putting a hand over his mouth. He smelled like vomit and blood, his cheeks now a feverish red while sweat collected on his skin. "Shut up. Shut up! Please, just be quiet–"

Before I even had a chance to pull myself together, the tears were already coming down. It embarrassed me even though I knew it shouldn't. That view of Shane, crying so hard he couldn't breathe while his eyes screamed at me to make the pain go away, would always stay with me. I knew that, even then.

It wasn't fair. It just wasn't fair.

I tried to tell him to breathe, but nothing helped. My hand over his mouth was making his face turn colors. I pulled it away and he gave a sudden gasp, followed by a whine of pain. That sound, as small and impotent as it was, made all the difference. Shane's eyes darted around the tent as the sides began to shiver, pushed one way and then another by something that enveloped our entire sanctuary at once. He screamed when an outline of a large, crooked hand formed an indent against the thin plastic. It was looking for a way in.

One hand turned into two, then three, then four. I couldn't tell if this was one creature or many. Shane and I could hear its obsessive need to get in, woven in the angry shrieks from an inhuman mouth and the furious swipes of its claws. Again and again, it tore at the tent in every direction while circling in a blind panic. It seemed to match Shane's terror; it was as desperate to get to us as he was desperate to escape.

I pulled Shane toward me so that the creature wouldn't touch him, even as its weight began to collapse one side of the tent. When I cradled him like a baby on my lap, he shivered and gripped my shirt with one hand. His knuckles were bloody and white. In that moment, I realized that I was the only thing left that made him feel safe.

"When I unzip the side, we've gotta run, okay?" I said, holding Shane's shoulders tightly to make sure he listened. "As fast as you can, and do not look back. Hear me? Do *not* look back even–"

A terrible shriek came from above. Shane's face was contorted into a look of pure terror as something blocked out the moonlight, ripping into the netting above our heads. What was once a view to the stars was now an open window, and I was lucky enough not to see what Shane saw. Instead, I looked up just in time to spot a set of long, skinny arms reaching toward us. They were all different sizes, made of some rough texture between flesh and tree bark that I didn't have a name for. Some were vestigial and half-formed. They moved so quickly that I couldn't count them all.

I braced myself, covering Shane's body as best I could. But the thing didn't want me. I felt its cold, dry hands pull on the back of my shirt to lift me up, then toss me aside as if I weighed nothing at all. My head hit the ground, and blinding lights swirled behind my eyes for a few seconds. It was just long enough for Shane to get snatched from the ground and pulled head-first through the roof, his legs kicking wildly in all directions while his broken arm dangled and dripped.

Desperately, I leapt forward and grabbed Shane's feet, trying to pull him back down. He only screamed louder, now tugged in two different directions at once. I could feel warm blood against my skin as it dripped onto my face. The shiver that went up my spine was like a fever.

The creature pulled harder, and I was knocked down onto my ass as it stole Shane out of my grasp with a violent tug. I backed myself up into the corner of the tent, every inch of my body trembling as I screamed louder than I ever had in my life. Even when I broke my leg sledding three years earlier, even when I used to have night terrors as a little kid, I never screamed so hard that my throat nearly bled.

The creature held Shane in the air, his upper body outside of the tent while his legs were still flailing in front of me. I wanted to reach out and grab him again. I wanted to pull him back down. But then, I heard one last scream from Shane and a sickening *crunch*. It wasn't the sound of a breaking bone or snapped twigs. It was wet and thick and followed by a long, agonized tearing sound that reminded me of meat being pulled off the bone.

I watched Shane's body twitch and shiver. That's all it was now: a body. While I watched in silent horror, I could see the exact moment when Shane was no longer there, when the purposeful kicks turned to dying spasms.

When his cries and screams were gone, I only heard my own, mingling with the disgusting drip of fresh blood against the tent floor. It pooled beneath him, trickling over his clothes and his skin until the drops ran down the sides of his dirty old shoes.

Blinded by tears and lightheaded to the point of nearly passing out, I saw a brief, blurry glimpse of Shane's body being pulled through the roof entirely. His feet dragged against the top layer of plastic before the thing carried him off, taking huge strides and cracking branches as it went. It never looked at me. It didn't want me. That creature, its face unknown to me but its intentions clear, was gone in mere seconds, leaving only a puddle of blood and vicious claw marks behind.

I stayed in that tent for a long time, screaming into my backpack and too afraid to leave. Stuck in a cocoon of blood and viscera, I waited for the thing to come back and take me next, but it never did. Deep into the night, I thought I heard the voices of children crying. To this day, I don't know if it was a hallucination or that thing trying to torment me and lure me out.

Relief came in the early morning. A group of worried hunters had heard me screaming, and just before dawn, police officers were coaxing me out of the tent like a wounded animal. They put a blanket around me and had me sit in the bed of a truck, pulled out to the treeline where only the tractors drove. Somehow, that walk was so much shorter now. We weren't that far from the field.

Before my mom arrived to pick me up, I remembered snippets of conversation heard between the trees.

"Black bear, you think?"

"Probably. I'm sure the boys didn't know there was a den around here. Mama bear just tryin' to protect her cubs."

"Never seen a bear take a kid's head off in one clean bite, though. Any sign of the boy's feet?"

It was at that point that I covered my ears, not wanting to hear anymore. But even the muffled, unintelligible voices created visions that would haunt my dreams for life: images of what they must have found, what was left behind, what I would have seen if the moon was just a little bit brighter.

My mom was there in minutes, escorted by police. She told me that Dad was on the way, but I couldn't even find the energy to look at her. The whole time, as her arms circled around my shoulders and she rocked me back and forth like a baby, I was watching Mr. Webber pace back and forth at the edge of the field with his hands in his pockets. He didn't look devastated or pained the way most people might expect for a man who had just lost his only child. Instead, there was something else in his posture that stuck with me to this day: shock followed by a cold, tired resignation as he slowly accepted his transition from 'father' to 'just Keith'. Loneliness never fit someone so well.

After that night, I didn't go back to school. My mother quit her part-time job to homeschool me for the rest of the year, until the nightmares got too intense and therapy wasn't helping anymore. By the time they caught me putting newspapers over my windows, my parents were at their wit's end. A year after Shane died, we moved away and started over in a smaller house just outside the city. *A place where you can make a lot of new friends*, my parents said. I never did. The bullying and isolation I felt as an anxious, suicidal thirteen-year-old was a grim reminder of what Shane probably felt every day of his life.

Somehow, I ended up carrying his torch, just as my mother feared I would: shoplifting, getting into trouble, starting my journey with my dad's liquor cabinet and moving my way up to pills and then cocaine a few years later. None of it ever made the trauma go away, but it numbed the terror I still felt in the night. It made me stop thinking about him. About the woods.

But my hometown always called me back somehow.

Sometimes, when I went home and sat on the fence facing the woods, I got so lost that time fell away from me. Before I knew it, the afternoon had passed me by. A stinging pain brought me back. With a sharp breath, I winced and dropped my cigarette, which had burned all the way down to the edge of my cold, shaking fingers. I rubbed the ash on the thigh of my pants.

Watching the treeline made my stomach feel sick. Every shiver of wind, every creaking branch, every rustle of leaves took me right back to where the nightmare all started. It was right down the road from that house, not far from the trailer park where old Keith still lived, alone and drunk and dying. I heard a rumor that the old man had cancer, but didn't want treatment. I heard another rumor that he spent some time in jail after police poked around his place, but what they found always changed depending on who was telling the story.

And when I drove down the winding dirt road, I noticed the shoe tree got a little bigger every year.

After a five-minute drive, I stepped out and slammed my car door behind me, boots digging into the gravel. It was the same gravel we had ridden our bikes on years ago, only tossed around a little differently now. I fidgeted with my lighter while circling the tree, staring up at the swaying branches and the many pairs of child-sized shoes hanging from old, dying limbs.

Some looked new, others had been there for decades. Once in a while, flies would gather around, buzzing in and out of one pair of shoes in particular at any given time. And as my eyes wandered over the many mismatched pairs, I spotted a familiar pair of tattered soles and worn-out laces near the very top of the tree. The dark stains had long dried. They hadn't moved from that spot in almost thirty years.

The air got colder around me, and a wind from the forest blew a rotten stink into my face that was all too familiar. The woods remembered me. I knew it did. And when the wind died down and the crows stopped cawing, I swore I could still hear the cries and screams of children that would never come home.

Shane's old shoes trembled against the breeze, tapping together like gruesome windchimes. I don't think anyone will ever find the bones still left inside.